DEATH AT THE
VOYAGER HOTEL

Kwei Quartey

Afram Publications (Ghana) Limited

Electronic Edition by: K. A.B. Publishers
Pasadena, California, U.S.A.

Print Edition by:
Afram Publications (Ghana) Limited
P.O. Box M18
Accra, Ghana

Tel:	+233 302 412 561, +233 244 314 103
Kumasi:	+233 322 047 524/5
E-mail:	sales@aframpubghana.com
	publishing@aframpubghana.com
Website:	www.aframpubghana.com

©Kwei Quartey, 2014

First Published, 2014
ISBN: 9964 70 522 0

Cover illustration by: Isaac Awuley Addico & Ellie Searl, Publishista®

Frontispiece by: Isaac Awuley Addico

In memory of Phylicia Moore

Prologue

In equatorial Africa, day breaks around 5:30 a.m. no matter the time of year. Morning preparations at the Voyager Hotel in Accra, Ghana, follow a similar timetable. The breakfast buffet is laid out, the day staff arrives to take over from the graveyard shift, the janitor sweeps the lobby, and tour buses and hired cars park in readiness at the front of the hotel.

Jost Miedema also has a set routine each morning. His alarm goes off at 5:40, and he rises and changes out of his pajamas. His busy schedule begins with a one-hour swim. Leaving his hotel chalet, he walks across the lawn to the pool, enjoying the feeling of the springy grass underfoot. A former triathlete, he's a healthy forty-five. To his left stands the main hotel, an oblong, two-story building painted a singular pink that glows in the dawn. Accommodations there are significantly cheaper than the chalet. Fortunately, his company pays for his luxury.

The solar lights around the pool deck are off, but there is already enough illumination from the sun's nascent rays. He tosses his towel onto one of the umbrella tables, pulls his goggles over his head and presses them against his eyes to make a tight seal. As he walks to the edge of the pool, he sees a shadow at the bottom of the deep end.

Thomas, the gardener, is unfurling the hose to water the canna lilies in the hotel's back garden. He is the first person to hear the cries for help. He drops everything and runs around the corner to the swimming pool, where he finds Mr. Miedema on the deck kneeling over a naked white woman and pumping her chest hard with both hands. She is ghostly pale except for her head and neck, which are purplish. Her arms and legs are flexed upward in the rigor of death.

"She's drowned!" Mr. Miedema screams at him.

"Go and get the doctor!"

Thomas turns around and begins to run as Amadu, the night security guard, comes rushing in the opposite direction.

"Call the doctor!" Thomas yells to him. "Somebody drown!"

Amadu rushes back to the hotel. As Mr. Miedema continues CPR, Thomas hovers, his hand over his open mouth as he exclaims in distress, "Ao! Ao!"

A spectator crowd, mostly hotel staff, is forming at one end of the pool. Thomas takes off his shirt and covers the woman's private parts.

Amadu returns with Dr. Franklin, a squat balding man still in his pajamas.

"What happened?" he asks, crouching beside Mr. Miedema.

"Found her at the bottom of the pool when I came to swim," he says, out of breath.

"Oh, my God," Franklin mutters. "I think she's long gone. Stop compressions a moment."

He palpates her neck with his fingertips, feeling for the carotid pulse. There is none. Her opaque eyes stare up without seeing and her body is as cold and lifeless as a stone statue.

He shakes his head sadly. "I'm sorry. We're too late."

1

*P*aula Djan looked up at the light tap on her office door and saw Ajua standing there. She was fourteen years old, tall for her age and a tough kid. Her eyes were beautiful, although they could cut deep into you and flare dangerously when she was angry. Now they were soft and anxious.

She curtsied imperceptibly. "Good morning, Madam Djan."

"Morning, Ajua. Come in. Something wrong?"

"Please," she said softly as she came forward, "will Madam Heather come today?"

"Yes. Why?"

"Please, I always meet her outside the school at ten minutes to eight, but up till now, she has not come."

"But Ajua," Paula said, smiling kindly, "it's only five past. She might be caught in traffic or something like that. You know how congested Accra is on a Monday morning."

"Please, she's never late," Ajua insisted.

"She'll be here," Paula said confidently. "Go and get ready for class."

"Yes, Madam."

Paula chuckled under her breath as she fondly watched Ajua leave. She was one of the success stories at the High Street Academy in Accra. Until Heather's arrival, no one had been able to put the brakes on Ajua's truancy. She was sleeping in class, failing all her tests, and on the verge of expulsion when Heather took her under her wing. She must have perceived some hidden potential in the girl, and something about this new teacher's aide from America had inspired Ajua. Heather put in extra time after school to tutor her, and now Ajua was a consistently C-student, an amazing transformation.

Paula was the headmistress of the High Street Academy, an urban school that provided free education to eight to fifteen-year-old needy children from nearby neighborhoods. It was a single building surrounded by the ramshackle homes that had sprung up behind the Accra Arts Center, a tourist trap on High Street; but it was an exceedingly rare tourist who knew about this humble school where teachers strived to change the lives of their young students—if not now, then in the future.

Heather was exactly the kind of worker Paula needed right now, because the school's performance during the last quarter had slipped. Only fifteen minutes ago, she had been on the phone with her boss, Kwame Coker, who had warned her that the school's Danish sponsors might withdraw funding by the end of the year if standards did not pick up. That gave Paula nine months to turn things around.

"They want to see better results," Coker had said emphatically. "Our target is one-third of the student body transferring to top junior high schools, particularly high-achieving girls. It's very important that our girls succeed."

"Yes, of course Sir," Paula had stammered, hearing the desperation in her own voice. "Believe me, no one wants them to succeed more than I do, but we're wrestling with teen pregnancy, the number one reason for girls dropping out; it isn't easy."

"Then you need to try harder," he said firmly. "Look, as director of the program, I must go to the Danes and say, 'here are the achievements for the year.' If I have nothing to show them, they're going to ask me why they should continue to give us money. That means my job, your job, all of our jobs, are on the line."

"Yes, Sir."

"So make this the first day of a new beginning. Clear?"

It was indeed to be the first day of a new beginning, but not in the way Coker had meant nor in a manner Paula would have imagined. When Heather had not shown by 8:45, Ajua's concerns no longer seemed unfounded. In a corner of the small room that doubled as administrative office and staffroom, Paula's assistant Gale was talking to a desk clerk at the Voyager Hotel. "I'm only asking if you would please go to her room and find out if she is there and whether she is okay."

Hotheaded Gale was petite and fair-colored, while her mostly unflappable boss was tall, dark, and well built. After listening to the clerk's unhelpful reply, Gale hung up in annoyance. "Agh. He says he's not allowed to provide that kind of private information over the phone. Aren't you good friends with the manager over there?"

"Yes—Edward Laryea," Paula said, scrolling through the contacts on her phone. "I'll call him now."

The number rang several times without a response, but there was still another option. "Take my car," she said to Gale, digging into her purse for the keys. "Go to the Voyager yourself, check if Heather is there and if she's all right. Who knows, she might be in bed with malaria or something."

"Okay," Gale said, grabbing the keys and disappearing through the door as swiftly as a sparrow.

During the years Paula had been at High Street Academy, she had been sending the foreign teachers' aides to stay at the Voyager Hotel. The accommodations weren't fancy, but the rates were good, and the place was scrupulously clean.

At nine fifteen, Paula was to meet with a journalist from the Ghana Herald newspaper, which was doing a series on the plight of Accra's burgeoning population of homeless children. Because the paper could be sensational and controversial, Paula had hesitated to do the interview, but had decided in the end that her refusal would have looked bad.

She looked up as Diane Jones came into the office. She was a chubby, black Chicagoan who, like Heather, was a volunteer teacher's assistant at High Street Academy. She

4

was usually cheerful, but today she was worried.

"Any word?" she asked Paula.

"No, but I've sent Gale to look for her." Paula said. She had a sickening foreboding. "Heather didn't mention anything to you about coming late today?"

"No," Diane said. "Last night, I told her I'd be coming in very early to get some paperwork done, and all she said was, 'okay, see you at eight.' I was up at five this morning and left the hotel around five thirty."

"It's not like her not to let me know if something is wrong," Paula said, frowning.

Oliver, one of the permanent staff teachers, came into the office. "Have you heard anything from Heather?"

"No," Paula replied, "but Gale has gone to look for her at the Voyager. Heather hasn't left any messages for you in the past few minutes?"

Fidgeting from one foot to the other, Oliver checked his phone screen again and shook his head. "Nothing."

His troubled expression said everything about how he was feeling. Of all people, he should have heard from Heather because he was dating her. Paula would have preferred that romances in the workplace never happened at all, but they were inevitable and impossible to stop. The only action she had taken was to make sure Heather and Oliver never taught together in the same class. Sidelong, yearning glances between them was not what a bunch of already excitable students needed.

Heather and Oliver were a fine study in contrast—she slim and strawberry blond with a heart-shaped face and aqua eyes, he broad and deeply black with flared nostrils and cheekbones like mountain ridges.

"I'm sure she'll be here," Diane said tentatively, but the questioning tone of her voice betrayed her. "I'll check back with you after this period."

Oliver had a class to teach as well, and his students had begun straggling in. Space was in short supply, such that his classroom abutted Paula's office. He left to begin the lesson, his brow still creased with worry.

"Take your seats," she heard him instructing the kids through the half-open door. "Quietly!"

Worn, rickety wooden desks and chairs scraped and squeaked, papers rustled, and the giggles and boisterous jostling died down. Paula stood unobtrusively at the door and watched Oliver teach the English class. It was the most difficult subject for many of the students. Math was less of a problem.

"Take out your pencils and exercise books, please," he said. "Let's see how well you have learned your spelling."

Two boys were clowning around in the back row.

"Come here," Oliver said tersely to them. "Both of you."

They came up meekly to the front of the class and he scolded them in English first, and then, for emphasis, in Ga. Addressing them in their mother tongue had more impact, and Ga, an innately sterner language than English, was well tailored for rebuke.

"You're not here to play, eh?" Oliver said. "You're here to learn so you can make something of yourselves. Do you understand?"

The boys kept their shorn heads bowed and made no eye contact with their teacher.

"Go and sit down," he said. "No more playing the fool.

Oliver gave them a shove, but as they returned to their seats, Paula could see the secret twinkle in his eye. He was very fond of the children, and concern for their wellbeing and ultimate success lay beneath even his strongest reprimands. That was why Paula had hired him. He was a good teacher, first, but just as important was his caring nature.

A man Paula didn't know was approaching the office from alongside the classroom. Guessing he was the journalist, she opened the door wide to welcome him.

"Mrs. Djan?" he asked as he reached her.

"Yes, good morning."

"I'm John Prempeh with the Ghana Herald."

She invited him in. He was short and wide, with a round, boyish face and spectacles.

"I hope this is an okay time for you?" he asked deferentially.

"It's fine," she said, nodding, "although there might be one or two interruptions—either by the staff or the kids, or phone calls."

"No problem."

They sat down and Prempeh took out a small recording device and put it on the desk between them. His newspaper had already published the first segment of his two-part series on the homeless, out-of-school children who roamed Accra's streets selling small items, dismantling electronic waste, and doing odd jobs.

"Thank you for seeing me, Mrs. Djan," he said. "The first question I have is about the composition of the High Street Academy students."

"We have about one hundred and twenty children attending," she said. "They come from poor Accra neighborhoods, particularly Jamestown. We admit students at Beginner, Intermediate and Advanced levels, depending on their prior level of schooling. Many have dropped out or missed school because of poverty or family strife."

Prempeh made a note of that on his yellow legal pad. "Is the education completely free?"

"Books and supplies are one hundred percent financed by a Danish NGO," she said, "and the students get lunch every day, Monday to Friday."

"I see." He looked up again. "How large is your staff?"

"We have four teachers, and two volunteer teacher assistants from the States, and then there's my assistant and me. I can stand in for any of the teachers if need be."

Prempeh repositioned his glasses, which had been steadily sliding down his oily nose. Paula thought he seemed nice enough.

"What are some of your success stories among the children?" he asked her.

"We've transferred several of our brightest to the best middle and junior high schools in the country," Paula said proudly.

"What proportion of the entire student body are these brightest children?"

This was the sensitive part, and Paula chose her words carefully. "It has varied. Last year, we sent twenty-five of our kids to the most excellent schools. We aim for a higher percentage of course, but we're faced with problems of spotty attendance, truancy and teenage pregnancy. These factors work against us."

"So, about twenty percent, would you say?" Prempeh said. He sounded neutral, but Paula sensed he was leading up to something.

"Yes, but I emphasize those were the children who went to the best schools with the most stringent requirements," she said, somewhat defensively. "Other children were placed in second tier schools."

"Is it easy to get support from western countries?" he asked, now looking at her from over the top of his spectacles.

"No," she said regretfully. "All foreign donors have become stricter with their funds, and they now demand that certain criteria are fulfilled in order for the sponsorship to continue. We have to show results if we want to keep the money coming in."

Abruptly, Prempeh's expression changed from open to critical. "Don't you think that your relationship with these Danish donors fosters Ghana's continuing dependency on foreigners' handouts?"

She pulled back a little at the loaded question. "That's a subject of debate, but while we're wasting time arguing about it, Mr. Prempeh, I'm not going to sacrifice those kids outside in that classroom."

Her phone rang, and she was thankful to get away from

a potential argument with Prempeh. "Excuse me." The screen showed Edward Laryea was calling. "I need to take this. Hello, Edward?"

"Hi, Paula," he said. "I saw you called earlier, but I was tied up. It's about Heather Peterson, isn't it?"

Fleetingly, Paula thought Edward might have good news, but then she recognized the sober tone of his voice, and apprehension quickly took over.

"Something terrible has happened," he said.

Her stomach plunged and she felt faint.

"I'm so sorry," he said. "Heather was found dead this morning in the hotel pool."

2

$\mathcal{P}$aula was still shaking from the shock.

"She was only twenty-four," she told Detective Chief Inspector Agyekum, a fiftyish, bone-thin man with spidery fingers. He wrote everything down in his notebook.

The office door was shut for privacy. He had helped himself to a chair, but Paula had remained standing. For the moment, the schoolchildren were in the playground oblivious of the tragedy. Paula knew that she would soon have to call assembly to break the horrifying news, and she dreaded the prospect.

"Did you see her over the weekend?" Agyekum asked Paula. His voice was thin, like a river reed. He had a plodding air and could have been either a dullard or a genius.

"No," she said. "We seldom got together on Saturdays or Sundays unless we had a special school event."

"I see." He studied her. "The last time you saw her was Friday afternoon, then?"

"Yes, Sir."

"Was she acting normally?"

"The same Heather we always knew. Happy, laughing, cracking jokes, helping the students in the classroom. They loved her. We all did."

As the DCI jotted down his notes, Paula gazed out of the window. She felt as if her chest had been hollowed out. The day had taken on a nightmarish quality. Heather had drowned to death. How could that be?

"Do you know if Miss Peterson could swim?" Agyekum asked, breaking into Paula's thoughts.

"Yes, very well," she said emphatically. "She often swam in the Voyager pool or at the beach, which is why I don't understand how she could have drowned. What exactly happened, Chief Inspector? Do you know?"

He finished what he was writing before answering her, as if he didn't like to do two things at once. "The medical examiner will have the final word when he does the postmortem, but our first impression is that it was an accident. Maybe she wasn't such a good swimmer after all and found herself unable to handle the deep end of the pool."

"But she was a good swimmer," Paula protested. "That's what I'm telling you."

He shrugged. "Even good drivers have car crashes."

That annoyed her somewhat—not what he had just said, but how he had said it.

"How deep is the pool?" she asked.

"About two meters. At least, that's what the hotel

manager told me."

"How long had she been in the water when she was found?"

"We don't know yet," he said, shaking his head slowly. "Did Miss Peterson drink alcohol or use drugs?"

"She drank beer and wine on occasion, but not heavily, and she definitely did not use drugs."

"All right." He stared at Paula again for a moment, as if pondering something. "I would like to talk to"—he looked at his list—"Diane Jones. Please have her come in."

Mrs. Djan left and sent in Miss Jones. She seemed dazed as she entered. She sat down as if bereft of energy. She looked completely deflated and gave Agyekum her full name and contact information in a soft monotone as she stared at the ground.

"When was the last time you saw Miss Peterson?" he asked her.

"Saturday afternoon at the Voyager," she said, voice flat, head down, shoulders slumped. "I stay there too."

"Seems like that hotel is very popular with the staff here," he commented.

"Paula arranges for all the teacher's aides to get a discount when we stay there," she informed him.

"Ah, I see." In return for her sending all her aides his way, he supposed. "So, on Saturday, you spent time with her?"

"We were together for a couple of hours by the pool. When it started to get dark, we went back to our rooms."

"Did she tell you about any plans for the night?"

"She said she would probably be going out."

"To where?" he asked with interest.

"She didn't tell me and I didn't ask."

Not like a woman not to ask, he thought. "Was she going to meet someone?"

Diane hesitated slightly. "She didn't say."

He pursed his lips and studied her. "Are you sure?"

"Yes, I'm sure."

A fly had gotten into the room and he swatted at it as it zigzagged around his head. "Did you and Heather swim while you were at the pool on Saturday?"

"She did, mostly," Jones said. "I dipped my legs in at the shallow end, but that's as far as I go. I can't swim at all. "

He jotted down, *Jones – can't swim,* with an asterisk. "Was Heather in the habit of swimming late at night?"

"Sometimes, yes—to cool off. She didn't like to use the a-c because it bothered her sinuses, so on hot nights, she went to the pool for about thirty minutes."

"This is March," he pointed out. "Every night is hot in Ghana around this time. Did Miss Peterson go to the pool every night?"

"I'd say often," Jones said uncertainly. "If not every."

"You didn't see her go to the pool last night, or hear her swimming?"

"No. You can't hear anyone swimming from the rooms— at least I can't, especially with the air conditioner on. Plus, at night the windows are shut to keep out the mosquitoes."

"Did Heather swim naked sometimes?" he asked, interested to observe Jones's reaction.

She was visibly startled. "What?"

"Naked. Did she swim naked?"

"No," she said, looking offended. "Why do you ask that?"

"Because that's how she was found in the pool—naked."

"Oh, my God." She put her hand to her mouth and tears welled up. He could see she was genuinely upset.

"Sorry," he said, regretting his bluntness, although he thought it was plausible that an American woman would do something like go swimming in the nude. He'd heard that people did that in the US, including having special beaches where you could walk around naked. Appalling, he thought. He waited a moment before continuing "What time did you go to bed last night, Miss Jones?"

She thought back briefly. "About midnight."

"Between the time you were with Miss Peterson on Saturday afternoon," he said carefully, "and the time you went to bed last night, did you see her anywhere or have any contact with her?"

"No, I didn't."

"Did you wake up at any time during the night?"

"No—not for any significant period, at least."

"Did Miss Peterson drink?"

"When? While we were at the pool?"

"Yes—or any other time."

"She had a beer every once in a while, but not that afternoon. Why, did someone say she was drunk?"

"Did you ever see her intoxicated?" he asked, ignoring her question.

She frowned. "No."

"What about drugs - marijuana, cocaine, and so on—did

15

Miss Peterson take any?"

Diane shook her head firmly. She appeared a little annoyed by the questions, and that in turn seemed to have livened her up somewhat. "She wasn't that kind of person. Why, are you suspecting her of drugs or something?"

"No, Miss Jones, I am not," he said, a trifle impatiently. "Did Heather have a boyfriend?"

He noticed her eyes fluttered slightly at that. "Well, I guess she and one of the teachers here were dating," she said, "but I didn't get into her business."

"Which teacher?"

"Oliver Danquah."

Agyekum hadn't spoken to Mr. Danquah yet. "Did he and Heather get along well with each other?"

She shrugged. "They were dating, so they must have been, right? Like I told you, I didn't stick my nose in her business."

He was skeptical of that claim, because he'd never met a woman who minded her own business.

"Where was Miss Peterson from?" he asked.

"Portland, Oregon."

"How long had she been at High Street Academy?"

"Four months. She was going to stay a total of six."

"And yourself? How long?"

"I've been here seven months and I'll be staying another two. It's my second visit to Ghana."

"You like it?"

"Yes, I do."

He smiled at her. "Thank you, Miss Jones."

He held the door open for her.

Oliver Danquah, well built and stylishly dressed, looked morose and tense.

"I'm sorry for your loss," Agyekum said.

"Thank you, Sir."

"I understand she was your girlfriend."

"Yes, Sir."

"When was the last time you saw her?"

"Yesterday." A faraway look came to his eyes as he recalled. "After church, I went to meet her at the hotel around noon. We went to the Accra Mall to see a movie, and then to Shoprite. After that, we ate at one of the restaurants."

"Was that all you did?"

"Yes, Sir."

"Did she plan to swim in the evening?"

"I don't know," he said, appearing distracted. "I don't think so."

"Did you go back to the Voyager Hotel with her after leaving the mall?"

"Yes, Sir."

"And then?"

Danquah looked puzzled. "And then what?"

"That's what I'm asking you," Agyekum said with a one-sided smile. "After you and Heather returned to the hotel, what did you do?"

Danquah shrugged. "Nothing."

"How nothing? Mr. Danquah, if you had sex with her, just say so. If you watched TV with her, then say it. None of this is a crime. Why are you evading my questions?"

"But I didn't have sex," he protested. "We talked, that's all."

"Okay," Agyekum said resignedly. "When is the last time that you saw her alive?"

"I left her around eight thirty to go to Korle Bu Hospital. My father is sick in the fever unit."

"You stayed with him for how long?"

"About one hour."

"And then where did you go?"

"Home. To sleep."

Agyekum eyed Danquah a moment. The man didn't only seem grief-stricken, he seemed nervous as well. "Where do you live?"

"Teshie."

"Can someone confirm that you came home and slept there through the night?"

"My roommate was there, but he was sleeping by the time I came in and he left the house for work by four in the morning."

"Do you sleep in the same room?"

"No, Sir."

"Was the door of your room open?"

"No, I always close it so he won't disturb me when he gets up."

"So he could not have seen that you were sleeping in your room and he can't vouch for you."

"Yes, Sir. He can't."

Agyekum paused his questioning to write a few items down in his notebook. "Mr. Danquah, did you go out again during the night, after returning to your house?"

"No, Sir. I told you I went to sleep."

"I know you told me that, but after you went to sleep, did you wake up again during the night to go somewhere?"

"Somewhere like where?"

"Anywhere, Mr. Danquah," Agyekum said. "Did you, for example, return to the hotel to sleep with Heather?"

"No," he said, giving Agyekum a wary look. "Not at all."

"Okay, so what time did you wake up in the morning?"

"Six o'clock."

"Were you having any problems with Heather? Any arguments or quarrels?"

Danquah's eyes darted to one side. "No, Sir. Everything was fine."

"You say everything was fine? Are you sure?"

"Yes."

Agyekum's eyes narrowed. "Please, Mr. Danquah—you need to answer my questions fully."

"I am," Danquah said, a defiant edge creeping into his voice.

"All right. Did you used to swim together in the pool with Heather?"

"Sometimes."

"Did she swim well?"

"Very well."

"What about you? Do you swim well?"

"Not so much."

Agyekum finished his notes. "Thank you very much. That's all for now."

Agyekum watched the handsome young teacher leaving the room and wondered if perhaps he had been too harsh with him. He had, after all, just lost his girlfriend.

When the chief inspector had left, Paula held a meeting in the office with the staff to discuss how they were going to break the news to the children. It was decided to divide them up by age group and assign each cluster to a teacher. That would be more intimate and personal than Paula simply standing in front of the assembly and making an announcement.

"Okay," she said to the teachers finally, when the plan had been all worked out, "go out there and be strong for our kids."

They filed out of the office, leaving Paula to reflect for a moment on what was happening. It felt unreal.

"Madam Djan?"

Paula turned at the soft voice at the door. It was Ajua.

"Madam Djan," she said again. "What has happened to Miss Heather?"

"Come," Paula said.

As she approached, Ajua's chin quivered and her eyes reddened in advance of the first tears that would break the dam. Somehow, she knew something was terribly wrong. Blessed or cursed, she possessed that kind of intuition. Paula held her tight as the girl began to weep.

3

At the end of an awful day of shock and grief, Paula was drained, but she felt that she had one more duty before heading home: she had to talk to Oliver alone. She called him into the office and shut the door. He still looked shattered as he slumped into the chair at the side of her desk.

"How are you doing?" she asked him softly. "Will you be okay tonight?"

He gave a tiny shrug.

"Maybe you should stay with a family member," Paula suggested, "so you'll have someone to talk to?"

He nodded. "I'll be going to my brother's house."

"Good." She paused. "I'm so sorry, Oliver. I know Heather meant a lot to you."

He was staring vacantly at the wall. "I don't know what to think…what to say."

"Did you see her yesterday?"

"Yes."

"And she seemed okay?"

"She was fine," he said dully.

Paula sensed this wasn't the time to ply him with questions. Maybe later. His head was in a fog right now.

"Shall I drop you at your brother's place?" she offered.

"No, thank you. I'll be okay."

"You can take the rest of the week off, if you like."

"It's better I work," he said, shaking his head. "It will keep my mind occupied."

"All right, then. But if you want some time, just let me know. Otherwise, I'll see you tomorrow. Call me if you need to."

"Thank you."

He got up slowly, as if he had aged decades in just one day.

◆ ◆ ◆

When she got home, Paula tried to phone Heather's father, Michael Peterson, in Portland, but he didn't pick up. She left a message. Heather had often spoken about her father, and in glowing terms. On the single occasion she had mentioned her mother, she had revealed that Glenda Peterson suffered from debilitating multiple sclerosis. It had appeared to Paula that it was a painful topic for Heather.

By the time Paula's husband Thelo got in from work, she had put their eight-year-old twins Stephan and Stephanie to bed after reading to them. Paula and Thelo had been secondary school sweethearts who had never considered marrying anyone else but each other. Four years younger than his thirty-nine, she was a social worker by training while he was an ex-detective sergeant with the Criminal Investigations Department, a division of the Ghana Police Service.

In his eighth year on the force, disaster befell Thelo as he and two other detectives pursued a car being driven recklessly by a fugitive wanted for murder. Rounding a sharp corner, the suspect ditched the car and the police vehicle came around too fast to avoid a collision. It flipped onto its side and rolled twice. The constable who had been driving and the chief inspector accompanying Thelo were both killed. The murderer got away, although he was later captured in another city.

As for Thelo, his lower right leg was crushed under the weight of the overturned vehicle. Several times in the following months, he had come perilously close to an amputation, which was averted only by a determined doctor who refused to give up. In the end, Thelo kept his leg, but the trauma resulted in loss of bone and left him with a limp that had improved only somewhat over the years.

The physical scar was ultimately not as damaging as the psychological one. Thelo grieved for his dead fellow officers, of whom he had been very fond. He felt guilty that they had died while he had escaped with his life. He had repeated nightmares of the crash. When he returned to police work, he found he had a difficult time concentrating. He was physically deconditioned and at times his right leg flared up with red-hot pain. Often, he was frustrated by having to stay in the office rather than go out to the field, which had always been his escape from the stifling bureaucracy of the CID. Depression hung around his spirit like a damp mist off the Atlantic. At the time, Paula was pregnant with the twins and she found herself despairing of Thelo's downward spiral. Then, one day, in a brilliant flash of inspiration, he turned to her and said. "I have to leave."

"Leave? Leave what?"

"The police service. God has been sending me a message, but I've been ignoring it."

What was Thelo planning to do? He had been following the 2007 discovery of substantial oil reserves off Ghana's coast and the promise of potential prosperity. He founded Tropical Expeditions, a full-service tourist company. In the early days of Thelo's business when revenue was barely trickling in, life was a struggle, particularly with two small children.

Now, however, he was doing very well with an office each in Accra and Takoradi. He and Paula owned a four-bedroom house and two cars in the upscale Airport Residential Area, and their daughters went to one of the best private schools in Accra.

Paula could have lived a life of leisure, shopping and dining all day the way many of her wealthy friends did, but she suffered from consumer's guilt, as she called it: acquiring much from the world but never giving anything back. She had to do something besides merely indulging herself, and four years ago when she heard that the High Street Academy was looking for a director, she interviewed for the post and got it.

Thelo threw his jacket aside in the sitting room and yanked off his tie. He had been slim as a detective, but now his belly bulged as a result of too much rich food and too little exercise. He shaved his head clean instead of displaying the hair loss that had begun by the time he had reached thirty.

Earlier in the afternoon, Paula had called him to give him a short version of the shocking news.

"Have they found out anything more?" he asked her, plopping down onto the sofa beside her.

"Chief Inspector Agyekum said they think it was a tragic accident," Paula said, "but that doesn't sound right to me. What was Heather doing in the pool naked? She would not have gone swimming without her clothes on."

"I agree," Thelo said. "She didn't seem to be that type of person."

Paula leaned forward with her elbow on her knee and her chin in her palm. She sighed, shaking her head.

He gently rubbed her back. "You've had a terrible day. Did you tell the students the news?"

"I had to. I didn't want them to hear it from elsewhere."

"How did they take it?"

"Very badly. They all loved her. You remember Ajua, the one who had become especially attached to Heather? She was hysterical—almost collapsed."

"Poor thing."

Paula's eyes misted over. "This has been the worst day of

my life—except when my father died."

Her phone rang, showing an overseas number. "Oh, this might be Mr. Peterson," she said, sitting up quickly. "Hello?"

The male voice was gravely. "Is this Paula Djan?"

"Speaking."

"This is Mr. Peterson, Heather's father." He paused. "I've already heard the news. The detective in charge of the case got in touch with me by phone – Inspector Adgie-something. I'm not too clear on his name."

"Agyekum," Paula prompted. "Mr. Peterson, I don't know how to express how very sorry I am. All of us at High Street Academy are in a state of complete shock."

"Yes," he said. His tone was flat. "Thank you."

"Heather was wonderful with the children and they adored her," Paula went on, her voice trembling. "They all said they never wanted her to go back to the States."

"She talked a lot about the kids," he said, now sounding very sad. "She said she wished she could adopt one of them. She seemed happy, but now this. I just don't understand. The inspector was saying she drowned? How could she have drowned? She taught swimming lessons in Portland every summer. She swam in the ocean. Are you kidding me? I mean, you saw the superb shape she was in. I'm sorry, but none of this makes any sense."

"It doesn't to me either."

"It wasn't an accident," he said, his voice growing sharper. "Someone either drowned her and left her in the pool, or killed her elsewhere and then threw her in."

Paula swallowed hard. The thought was horrifying.

"I never wanted her to go to Ghana," he continued. "I had a bad feeling about it."

"I'm so sorry," Paula said helplessly. She didn't know what else to say.

"I mean, I'm not saying anything against you specifically," he hastened to add.

"Yes, I know, but I feel terrible."

"I expect to be in Ghana Friday morning to make arrangements for Heather to be flown back home," he said, sounding weak and battered. "I spoke to the people at the American Embassy in Accra, and they'll be able to help with that, and I want to get the FBI involved in the investigation, too."

"Oh." Paula hadn't thought of anything like that. "Did you mention the idea to Chief Inspector Agyekum?"

"I did," Peterson said. "He didn't really respond. I know the FBI goes to other countries when there's some kind of suspicious death of an American citizen – like they did in the Natalee Holloway case in Aruba."

"I see," Paula said. She knew nothing about it. "Well, I can ask my husband if he can help in any way. He used to be a homicide detective here in Accra."

"Really? Yes, if there's anything he can do, please let me know. Thank you, Paula."

"You're very welcome."

"What am I helping whom with?" Thelo asked her after she had hung up.

"Mr. Peterson is convinced his daughter's death was due to foul play," she said thoughtfully. "He says she was a very good swimmer and therefore can't believe she accidentally drowned. He wants to get someone from the FBI to come to Accra – I guess to help with the investigation, or supervise it, or something."

Thelo gave a small snort of derision. "Spoken just like an American. He thinks the FBI can just march in and take over the case? The Ghanaian authorities have to request assistance first, and knowing the Director-General of CID, I can practically guarantee he won't. He has a brand new, state-of-the-art forensic lab and crime scene unit, the lab director himself trained at Quantico at Ghanaian taxpayer expense, and now he's going to turn around and ask the FBI for help? The media would have a field day."

"You're right," she agreed. "What do you suggest Mr. Peterson should do?"

Thelo held up his right index finger. "The first thing is to wait for the autopsy result, then go from there. It's premature to be talking about the FBI and all that."

"But I do understand his bewilderment," Paula said. "He knows his daughter well. She was a strong swimmer and even taught swimming, so how could she have drowned in two meters of water? And why was she naked? It makes no sense."

"Wait for the autopsy," Thelo said firmly. "Let's not jump to conclusions."

4

*O*n Thursday, having done little or no paperwork in the past three days, Paula went to the office early to try to make some headway writing up the goals for the next quarter. She had been working twenty minutes when her phone rang. It was Chief Inspector Agyekum.

"Good morning, Chief Inspector."

"Good morning, Mrs. Djan. I have some news regarding the death of Miss Heather Peterson."

"Yes?" she said tentatively.

"The medical examiner has done the autopsy and found no signs of foul play. However, Miss Peterson's blood alcohol concentration was very high, so it appears that she had a lot to drink prior to entering the pool. We therefore conclude that this was an accidental death, and that she most unfortunately drowned as a result of being highly intoxicated."

Paula was stunned. "Highly intoxicated? I don't

understand. Heather was not a heavy drinker. In fact, she drank very little."

"Could it be simply that you never witnessed her drinking heavily?"

She thought she detected some sarcasm in his tone.

"But no one else has reported her drinking heavily either," she objected. "Otherwise, I would have surely heard something about it."

"Sometimes the findings at autopsy come as a shock to the loved ones of the deceased," he said. Maybe he was trying to be sympathetic, but it only sounded condescending to Paula.

"But why was she naked in the pool?" she demanded, hearing her voice rise. "Can you explain that?"

"Please, Mrs. Djan, as I'm sure you know, alcohol reduces one's inhibitions. I have seen many strange things as a result of alcohol consumption. This is not the worst of them."

"Maybe you can imagine Heather taking off all her clothes to swim naked," she said heatedly, "but I cannot. Are you sure this isn't some kind of mistake? Maybe her blood sample was accidentally switched with someone else's?"

"Oh, no, I don't think so," he said, and Paula could hear him smiling in tolerant amusement, which annoyed her.

"Something doesn't fit, Chief Inspector," she said emphatically. "I just know something is wrong." He didn't comment, and that aroused her suspicions. "I think you sense it too. I think you know something is wrong but your superiors at CID would much rather drop this. I know how it works over there. They've instructed you not to go any further, am I not correct?"

"The case will be officially closed by the day's end," he answered decisively.

"Please, you didn't answer my question." She felt desperate. "Your higher-ups ordered you to discontinue the investigation, didn't they?"

"No, Mrs. Djan. I'm very sorry for the bad news. Goodbye."

She sat staring at her desk without seeing, and jumped as Gale came in.

"Morning, boss." She stopped in her tracks. "What's wrong?"

Paula looked at Gale in disbelief. "I've just gotten off the phone with Chief Inspector Agyekum. He says the conclusions from the autopsy are that Heather drank heavily and became so intoxicated that she went swimming naked in the pool and drowned."

"No!" Gale exclaimed, dropping her backpack on the floor. "Heather? How can that be? I've never seen her drink to excess. Have you?"

"Certainly not on the two occasions we socialized. The first time she was at my house was when we had the Sunday lunch for the staff, and she might have had one beer at the most. The second time was that Saturday evening to celebrate her birthday—remember?"

"Yes," Gale said, nodding. "She had a glass of champagne—said it was sweet the way she liked it, and that she wasn't much of a drinker."

"I'm sure there's more to this story," Paula said. "How

can Chief Inspector Agyekum not see how strange it is that Heather was found naked?"

"He doesn't know her the way we do."

"Well, did he ask what she was like?" Paula asked sharply. "No, he did not. What kind of detective is he?" She brooded for a moment. "And this is going to drag Heather's name through the mud. People will say, ah, well, she suffered the consequences of swimming while drunk. And what in heaven's name are they doing over there at that school? Some alcoholic woman coming from America to teach our children? Swimming naked in a public area? You know, we don't like that kind of thing in Ghana."

Gale sucked her teeth three times in rapid succession as she imagined the troubling scenario.

"And then we have the kids to worry about," Paula said in growing dismay as all the implications began to dawn. "Especially Ajua. How is she going to respond when people start asking her about the teacher who swam in the pool naked and then drowned?"

"And we're struggling to keep this Danish grant going, too," Gale said heavily. "Bad publicity is what we don't need."

"We have to do something," Paula said.

"What?"

"I don't know yet." Paula got up and paced the distance the small room would allow. "But we will do something."

Mid-morning, John Prempeh called Paula to ask her if she had a statement to make on the death of Heather Peterson. Paula had prepared herself for media inquiries, but Prempeh was the last person she wanted to talk to.

"We're devastated and saddened by her death," she said. "She was a valued asset to the Street Academy. Because it's an ongoing investigation, I can't comment any further than that."

"Had she been drinking heavily?"

"Mr. Prempeh," she said sharply, "as I just said, I can't comment any further."

"What about the possibility that she committed suicide?"

"Nothing further, Mr. Prempeh. Good day." She ended the call in disgust.

At the end of the school day, Paula found Diane sitting alone at the teacher's desk in the first classroom marking students' papers. Paula asked her how she was feeling. Since Heather's death, she had been very quiet.

"I'm a little better, I think," she said, as Paula pulled up a chair. "I haven't been sleeping that well though, and I've been thinking of moving out of the Voyager. Every time I catch a glimpse of the pool, I feel sick to my stomach."

Paula noticed how her voice had lost much of its former fullness and resonance.

"Diane," she said, "the chief inspector called me this morning about Heather's autopsy and toxicology results."

Diane sat up straight. "What did he say?"

"They've concluded that Heather drowned accidentally. They claim she had a high alcohol concentration in her blood, so they think she drank heavily, went swimming and drowned because she was so intoxicated."

Diane pulled her head back sharply, as if someone had tried to prod her in the face with a garden fork. "What?

Intoxicated! But she didn't drink that much. And no way she'd go swimming in the nude. What kind of crappy investigation is this?"

"That's what Gale and I were saying to each other this morning," Paula said in agreement. "We've been asking ourselves, have we missed something? I feel like we have. Did you see Heather on Sunday?"

"No, only Saturday afternoon. We hung around the pool for a while and then went back to our rooms when the light started to fade."

"Was she downcast about something?" Paula asked. "Did she say whether she and Oliver were having any problems?"

Diane looked uncomfortable and dropped her gaze.

"What's wrong?" Paula asked.

"The police inspector asked me if Oliver and Heather had been getting along well, and I answered that I thought they were, but that isn't true. On Saturday, while Heather and I were talking by the pool, she said she needed some advice on something. She told me in the time she'd been seeing Oliver, he'd gone from asking her to help him to get to the States to asking whether he could accompany her when she went back home to Portland, and finally to proposing marriage to her."

Paula's eyebrows shot up. "Go back to Portland with her," she echoed. "Marriage? What was Oliver thinking?"

"That was essentially Heather's question. Honestly? I think she started something she would never have been able to finish properly. The way I saw it, she was less in love with Oliver than with the novelty of being with a black man."

Paula was surprised. "Oh? Why do you say that?"

"I'm sure I'm not the only one who's noticed these white women who come to Ghana and get all swept up by the whole African virility myth. You know, all that jungle fever nonsense."

Diane's tone was bitter and she was frowning in distaste. Paula had never seen this judgmental side of her, and she was shocked.

"And on the other hand," Diane continued, "Oliver had ulterior motives in their so-called relationship."

Paula was puzzled by these analyses. "You don't think he was in love with her either?"

"In a way, but…"

"You don't trust him? I mean, what exactly are you saying?"

"I guess that's it," Diane said with a shrug. "I don't trust him."

Paula watched her for a moment as she brooded. "Let me ask you something, Diane. It's very personal, so you don't have to answer if you don't want to. Did you and Heather ever fight over Oliver?"

Diane sighed and put her pen down. "Okay, I'll tell you what happened. A while after I started working at High Street Academy, I got interested in Oliver. I mean, look at him. What red-blooded woman wouldn't be?"

Paula smiled slightly, but wasn't about to admit she agreed.

"But after I got to know him a little," Diane continued, "my character meter started sending me alarm signals. It's hard to explain; but at first, his focus seemed to be all about me; but then I realized that underneath it all, he's really all about himself. That's when I backed off and left him alone. Then Heather got here and I saw her falling for him, and I didn't like it—for her sake, I mean, of course.

"So, about a month ago," Diane went on, leaning back in her chair, "I was coming out of my room at the Voyager when I saw Heather going downstairs. She'd left her door ajar. As I passed it, I saw Oliver inside her room watching TV with his shirt off. He didn't see me. When I got downstairs, I bumped into Heather as she was coming back up. I don't know what got into me, but I blurted out to her that she shouldn't do anything she would later regret."

Diane shifted her position again and paused, wringing her fingers. "Of course, as soon as I said that, it was me who regretted it. Heather got upset and accused me of being jealous of her relationship with Oliver, and then we started bickering. Oliver heard us, and he came down the hallway to find us arguing. The whole thing was ugly and embarrassing, and I blame myself for starting it. But, you know, in the end, I was only concerned about Heather. That's all it was. I know it might have seemed like jealousy, but it wasn't."

"I see," Paula said understandingly, but she still wasn't certain that no jealousy had been involved. Diane's head might be saying that, but Paula doubted her heart was.

"So anyone suggesting I had it in for her," Diane said

with a weak grin, "don't pay them no mind."

"Anyone like whom?" Paula asked curiously.

Diane shrugged. "Oh, I don't know. Anyone."

Perhaps she really meant Oliver, Paula thought. She put a gentle hand on Diane's shoulder. "Are you going to be okay? Is there anything I can do to help?"

"No, nothing." Diane smiled at her. "You've done a lot already to help me get through this. Thank you."

It looked like she wanted to say something else, but was hesitant.

"What is it?" Paula asked encouragingly.

"D'you think Heather was murdered?

Paula gazed at the floor for a moment to frame her thoughts, and then looked up. "It isn't something we like to think about, but what we know about Heather doesn't fit the picture the police are trying to paint, and so I reject it. I've been casting around for explanations, but each time I come up with the same answer: there must have been foul play."

Diane was studying her closely. "That's a relief in a weird way. Just like you, I can't see Heather being responsible for her own death. I mean, all this stuff about going swimming while drunk...there's just no way."

Paula nodded. "Agreed."

"But are we going to be able to convince the police of that?"

"I don't know, but I'll come up with something. I just have to think about it."

"Okay—and if you need me to help persuade that chief

inspector again, let me know, because I'm happy to do it."

"Thank you."

"Meanwhile, I had an idea today," Diane said, brightening. "I want to put together a collage of all the pics I took of Heather as a tribute to her."

Diane was no professional photographer, but she loved taking photographs — particularly candid shots.

Paula jumped at the idea. "That would be wonderful! We'd all love to see it."

"I'll start working on it tonight.

Paula felt happy for Diane. She suspected that the collage would be a healing exercise for her.

After all the staff and students had left school, Gale came into the office to tidy up, moving around with the quick, efficient movements of a worker ant. She rarely stayed still and seemed to have inexhaustible energy.

"I spoke with Oliver this morning," she said, moving a stack of folders to wipe off her desk. "He's truly grieving over Heather. I feel so sorry for him."

"Me too," Paula said feelingly. "I offered him some time off, but he said he preferred to work. It can't be easy for him. Did he tell you anything new about Heather?"

Gale returned the stack to her desk and started on the bookshelves. "I asked him if he had picked up any signs on Sunday afternoon that she was sad or depressed about anything. He said no, that they went shopping together at the mall and she seemed to be in good spirits."

Paula began to help Gale by removing books and folders from the shelves. "I did learn something new from Diane, though. On Saturday afternoon while she and Heather were sitting together by the pool, Heather admitted that Oliver had been asking her to help him get to the States. He even proposed marriage to her."

"Marriage!" Gale exclaimed, pausing with her duster suspended. "Goodness."

"Diane says Heather was beginning to feel like the relationship was a mistake."

Gale began to slowly wipe the shelf off. "Is it possible that on Sunday night Heather told Oliver that she wanted to break up with him and they had a bad argument? So bad that Heather decided to get drunk to banish her sorrows? And then decided to go swimming?"

"I suppose anything is possible," Paula said, but doubtfully. "Did Oliver tell you how much time he spent with Heather that night?"

"Until eight thirty, and then he went to see his father who was in hospital."

"He didn't return to the Voyager after that?"

"No, he said he just went home." Gale tossed her duster onto the table in a gesture of frustration and sorrow. "I only wish none of this had never happened."

"I do too," Paula said. "Are you finished dusting here?"

"Yes," Gale said distractedly.

"Imagine what it must be like for Heather's father," Paula said, replacing the folders.

"A nightmare no parent wants to live through," Gale said, shaking her head. "When is Mr. Peterson arriving?"

"Supposedly tomorrow, if all goes as planned." Paula looked at her. "That's when the full reality will hit him. It's going to be very painful."

5

*T*he next morning, Friday, Gale burst into the office as Paula was getting set for the day.

"You won't believe this," she said, thrusting the Ghana Herald in front of her boss.

She had the paper opened to page three, and Paula read its headline. " 'High Street Academy Haunted by Death and Donor Fatigue.' By John Prempeh. What?"

"Oh, just read on," Gale said, arms folded, jaw set. "It gets worse."

" 'Accra's High Street Academy never had it so bad,' " Paula continued reading. " 'As Danish funding for the well-meaning project begins to dry up, the charity-supported school appears to have been cursed. The number of its teachers' aides falls short of what it should be. Suffering the brunt of the resulting increased work load, one of those aides, Heather Peterson, went into a deep depression, drank herself into oblivion and was found drowned and naked in a hotel pool last weekend as a result of severe intoxication.' "

Paula's blood had turned to ice. "Oh, my God. 'High Street Academy is another example of Ghana's addiction to handouts from the West and our fondness for securing funds for projects that never live up to expectations. High Street Academy's headmistress Paula Djan confesses that only twenty percent of the children being schooled ever make it to a public or private middle or junior high school.

" 'Twenty-four-year-old Miss Peterson, the drowning victim, was reportedly distraught over the long working hours and the almost unmanageable assignment load that the permanent, paid staff burdened her with for their convenience. A reliable source available to the Ghana Herald described Peterson as being depressed and having problems sleeping. Miss Peterson repeatedly complained about the "unruly and disobedient" street children in the school. Mrs. Djan either was not made aware of Miss Peterson's anguish, or neglected to take any action. Miss Peterson's nude state when she was found also raises a question about her mental stability.' "

"No!" Paula cried. "No!"

She read the article to the end, and then threw the paper down furiously. "Why is Prempeh doing this? 'Unmanageable assignment load that we burdened her with for our convenience?' That's a complete lie. Heather kept begging for more work than I was giving her. And 'raises a question about her mental stability?' How dare he!"

"Who is this so-called reliable source?" Gale asked. "Do

41

you have Prempeh's number? Because you should call him and give him a piece of your mind."

"Oh, I intend to," Paula said, "but first, we need to find out who told him that Heather was depressed, and whether it came from within these walls."

"Should I call a staff meeting?"

"Yes," Paula said grimly. "We'll hold it this afternoon after the children have gone home."

"I'll see to it, boss."

◆ ◆ ◆

Paula's phone rang. Her heart sank when she saw it was Kwame Coker calling. No doubt, he had just read the Ghana Herald article.

That afternoon, Paula addressed her staff members, who sat before her in a semicircle.

"We've had a terrible week," she began. "On Monday we met to talk about the shock we all experienced at the news of Heather's death. Today, the topic is different but related." She held up the Ghana Herald. "By now, we've all seen the article by John Prempeh. It's a reckless piece filled with lies – it's not even journalism. The Herald is notorious for this kind of sensationalism, and now I'm sorry that I spoke to the man at all. Mr. Coker read the article this morning and called me. He was furious and upset, and I'll tell you why.

"Our donors have been making the conditions for their continued support more and more stringent. Gone are the days when western countries tossed money at us without much thought. Now they want to see results. High Street

Academy must not only provide our underprivileged children with the best education possible, we need to show that we are successfully transferring at least one-third of the students to the top middle and secondary schools every year. Last year, we did not come anywhere close to that target."

Her gaze passed over each member of her audience. Their expressions were mostly neutral, but Diane's head was down, and so was Oliver's.

"There's something else," Paula continued. "We have to maintain a spotless image. The Danes are wonderful people, but they are also pragmatic. They have their own people to answer to. This report in the Herald gives an impression that we are lazy, that we have wild and uncontrollable children, and that we have been dumping inordinate amounts of work on our unpaid foreign workers. As if that weren't enough, Prempeh goes on to say that Heather became so depressed that she drank herself into near unconsciousness and then drowned. People reading this article will wonder what kind of hellish place we're running here."

As she said that, everyone turned glum and seemed to wither under the bleakness of the circumstances that had shattered the beginning of the week and grown exponentially worse by the end of it.

"The part of the article that worries me the most," Paula went on, "is where it says that Heather 'was described by a reliable source as being severely depressed and having problems sleeping.' I never saw any sign that Heather was severely depressed, and no one brought that to my attention if it was the case. Maybe I wasn't perceptive enough about Heather, or I missed something, but if one of you saw or knew something I failed to recognize, then I need to know. If the Ghana Herald deserves to know, so do I."

"Therefore, if this so-called reliable source is in this room and it is indeed true that Heather was so depressed that she drank to the point of dangerous intoxication, I appeal to whomever knew this to come to me with the truth. If a tragic mistake was made, if I neglected Heather in some way, I must learn exactly where I went wrong."

Now Paula saw uneasy fidgeting and furtive sidelong glances among the staff members. "I don't need anyone to say anything right now," she added, "but if one or more of you have something to tell me, I would like to hear from you privately, as soon as possible. Please feel free to call me over the weekend. Do you have any questions?"

One of the male teachers spoke up. "I never saw her looking depressed or sad." That sparked a burst of discussion within the group, everyone apparently denying that Heather had appeared troubled, and all saying that they had never told the newspaperman anything to that effect.

Paula noticed something else: Oliver and Diane were staring hard at each other, and she wondered what message was passing between them. Was it accusatory or conspiratorial? What secret was one or both of them hiding?

◆ ◆ ◆

Late afternoon, Paula was by herself in the office, her head in her hands. The staff and the kids had gone home. She had hated every minute of this week. While comforting others and allowing their grief to wash over her like a swirling tide, she had held herself together and never broken down. She had been the pillar of strength that the house needed to stay standing. But now she was alone, she released her emotions and quietly shed tears for Heather.

She lifted her head as she heard a noise outside. Hastily dabbing her eyes dry, she pulled herself together and opened the door to see who was there. Oliver was sitting at one of the student's desks, and was as surprised to see Paula as she was him.

"I thought you had gone home," she said.

"I went to get something to eat," he said, "but I came back here because it's quiet and I wanted to think."

She nodded. "I'll leave you alone if you like. Or do you want to talk?"

"Sure," he said. "Why not?"

She took a seat at the desk next to his. "How are you feeling?"

"Just…confused. My mind is tumbling over itself. I don't understand what has happened. How can Heather be gone? I was with her on Sunday, but now she's dead? How can that be?"

"It seems impossible," Paula agreed in sympathy. "I keep waking up at night thinking I've been dreaming it all and that Heather will be here at school in the morning."

He looked at her with anxiety in his eyes. "Did she…did she ever tell you anything bad about me?"

"About you?" Paula shook her head. "No. On the contrary.

She told me you made her feel loved and cherished."

"Really?" A smile crept to his lips and his expression turned soft as a memory came to him. "Once, when I took her to the Western Region, we were at the beach at sunset and she said it was like paradise there, and she hugged me and told me I was her Paradise Man. And from then on, whenever we were together, she said to me, 'what's up, my Paradise Man?'" A sound escaped from his throat that was a cross between a laugh and a sob. "That's why I don't understand how she was behaving on Sunday."

Paula sat forward a little. This was something new. "What do you mean?"

"I didn't tell you this before," Oliver said, looking uncomfortable, "but that day, she just wasn't herself. She was quiet, and when I asked her what was wrong, she just said, 'I'm okay.' I know her mother isn't well, so I thought maybe something bad had happened, but Heather said no. I took her to the Accra Mall to try and cheer her up. We watched a movie at Silver Bird and then we had some pizza – you know, she liked pizza a lot. After that, she seemed a little better, and we were walking around the mall when she saw a swimsuit in a shop there that she said she liked—kind of a tangerine color—so I bought it for her. She tried to stop me, but I insisted."

Paula knew that most prices at the mall were out of Oliver's budget range.

"And after the mall, did you go anywhere else?" she asked.

"No, we went back to the Voyager and spent part of the

evening together. I had to leave around eight-thirty to go and see my father at Korle Bu."

"So that was the last you saw of her."

He nodded, his head down. She squeezed his arm. "Just know that she thought the world of you."

"Sure?" he asked, with a suggestion of doubt that Paula didn't understand. Was there something else?

"What's troubling you?" she asked gently. "Are you harboring doubts?"

Eyes closed, he rubbed his forehead slowly. "I don't know. I'm mixed up, Paula."

She felt deeply sorry for him. He was so powerful physically, but he looked like a lost boy. "What can I do, Oliver? Tell me how I can help you."

He shook his head. "It's my battle. Thank you, Paula. You've always been good to me, and I appreciate it very much."

He was immersed in thought for a while, but then, as if suddenly waking from sleep, he stood up with what seemed a new burst of energy. Perhaps the little talk had helped.

"I'll see you on Monday," he said.

She reached for his hand and their fingers touched. "Get some rest tonight. I can tell you haven't been sleeping."

"I'll try," he promised, and walked slowly away.

Paula didn't want to wait until the evening to talk to Thelo, so she made her way to his office in East Legon, calling him to let him know she was on her way. It took her more than an hour. The Tropical Expeditions building was a single story with a glass façade revealing a spacious seating area for customers, and on one wall, a floor-to-ceiling carved map of Ghana with a different color wood assigned to each of its ten regions. Of the four desks supplied with laptops, three were occupied with agents and their clients. The youngest male, who was dressed smartly in a white shirt and black tie, stood up respectfully as Paula entered. "Good afternoon, Mrs. Djan. You are welcome."

"Thank you," she said, smiling and remembering him as one of Thelo's best workers. She continued to the rear of the room where the door to Thelo's office was to her left. She knocked and put her head in.

"Oh, there you are," he said, getting up from his desk. "Did the traffic monster swallow you?"

"Whole," she said, and then held up a copy of the Ghana Herald. "Have you read John Prempeh's article about High Street Academy?"

"No," he said, taking it from her. "You know I don't read this horrible paper."

She joined him on the sofa as he began to read. Thelo liked sleek, clean designs, and it showed in his uncluttered and airy office space and low-profile, ultra-modern furniture.

At intervals, he grunted as he went through the article, but as he got further, his exclamations became more expressive.

"This is disgusting," he said, shaking his head as he finished. "I've never liked that man Prempeh. Have you called him?"

"I've tried a few times today, but he doesn't pick up. He's

probably avoiding me. Thelo, we have to do something. He's ruining the name of both Heather and the school."

"Beyond protesting to him about it, what can we do?"

"We need to get to the truth to prove Prempeh wrong. Not only him, the medical examiner as well. It's simply not possible that Heather went swimming drunk and in the nude and then drowned accidentally."

"Maybe being drunk was the reason for the nudity."

"You've met her, Thelo. You know she wasn't some crazy party girl."

"So, what are you saying? That someone killed her and threw her in the pool?"

"Or drowned her deliberately, yes."

He was skeptical. "But how can you dispute the laboratory results showing a high blood alcohol level?"

"It must be an error," Paula said firmly. "I know it is. Can't we call the medical examiner or Chief Inspector Agyekum about it?"

"And say what? Order them to reopen the case? And he's just going to say, 'yes, massa?'"

"What about your friends at CID?"

"What friends?" he asked, flipping his palms up. "I was done with that place long ago."

"You still know quite a few people there."

"Paula, I can't tell them to revisit the case any more than they can tell me how to run Tropical Expeditions."

"No, no, no," she said, shaking her head vigorously. "It's not that you can't call them, it's that you can't be bothered. You can do anything you want to, Thelo. You recovered from your leg injury with sheer willpower, and you built all this"—she gestured around the room—"with determination alone, but you can't call your guys at CID? You know something? Running this business has really changed you, and not for the better. What happened to the detective I married who cared so much about justice and doing the right thing? That's what I loved and admired so much about you."

He started to say something, but apparently found himself at a loss. She saw his mind working as he wrestled with what she had just said.

"We just can't let this go," she pressed, sensing momentum. "If Heather's death wasn't really an accident, we're doing her a great injustice, and as an ex-detective, I expect you to be sensitive to that."

"Okay, okay—you've made your point."

"So you'll call someone at CID?"

"I didn't say that. I have to think it through first."

"Thank you. I appreciate it."

He looked pleadingly at her. "But in the time being, Paula, don't start calling people up, asking questions and snooping around, okay?"

"All right, I promise." She looked at her watch and stood up. "It's getting late. Do you want me to pick up the kids?"

"No, it's okay. I'm leaving in a few minutes and I'm going that way in any case. We'll see you later at the house."

◆ ◆ ◆

As Paula sat in traffic again, her certainty that Heather's

death had not been accidental grew even stronger.

"I'm going to find out who killed you, Heather," she murmured. "And I won't give up until I do."

6

On her way home, Paula passed through Adabraka, a suburb of Accra. As she waited at the wide cathedral intersection for the light to change, she reflected that the Voyager Hotel wasn't far away, and she wondered if Edward Laryea was there. Maybe she could drop by to talk to him. She had just promised Thelo that she wouldn't go snooping around, but this wouldn't really be that, she reasoned. It would be more like a friendly visit. She hadn't seen Edward in quite some time and it would be a nice gesture on her part to stop and say hello. As she got the green, she called his number and he answered.

♦ ♦ ♦

The hotel was a unique rusty pink that Paula had always found intriguing. She didn't know another building in Accra quite that color. Neatly clipped shrubbery lined the borders of the car park. A khaki-uniformed watchman sitting by his sentry box watched her pull into a perfect spot in the dappled shade of a Flamboyant tree.

Background music was playing as she entered the lobby, where a receptionist was busy with a guest at the curved front desk. A white couple was sitting on red faux leather armchairs in the seating area filling out forms. Stacked on the wall were magazines and tourist brochures, including some from Tropical Expeditions. The Voyager was a favorite with backpackers and other tourists on a limited budget, but the hotel now had three upscale chalets for customers who could afford it.

"Yes, Madam," the receptionist said to Paula after she had introduced herself. "Mr. Laryea is expecting you. You can go through to his office and I'll let him know you've arrived."

She walked down a short corridor, made a right, knocked on the door with Edward's name, and entered. He was at his desk in front of the computer. In his early forties, he was a mountain of a man. Paula and Thelo had known him since secondary school.

"Paula, my dear!" He jumped to his feet, towering over her. "Welcome, welcome. How unfortunate to meet under these circumstances."

He bent down to give her a quick hug and guided her to a pair of chairs to the side, where they sat opposite each other.

"It's been a tough five days," Paula said wearily.

"Terrible. Awful." Edward's brow creased. "Are you bearing up okay?"

"I think so, but the morale at Street Academy is low—very low."

He was sympathetic. "Here too. All of us have been wondering if there was something we could have done to prevent this tragedy. As general manager, I'm ultimately responsible, so it's been weighing heavily on me."

"I'm in much the same position," Paula said in commiseration. "I keep asking myself if I missed some kind of signal from Heather. Did you read that article by John Prempeh in the Ghana Herald?"

Edward made a noise of contempt with his mouth. "I saw it, but I don't believe a word of the bad things he said about you and the school."

"He claims he had a source who told him that Heather was depressed and having problems sleeping," Paula said. "If that's true, the source has to be someone closely associated with her. Did you ever see Prempeh here at the hotel talking to Diane Jones—or anyone else, for that matter?"

Edward turned his lips down at the corners. "No, I didn't, but if I hear something, I'll let you know."

"Thanks."

"What else can I help you with, my dear?"

"Thelo told me to mind my own business but I can't rest until I've asked a few questions. The police have rushed to close the investigation of Heather's death as quickly as they can, but I feel I simply have to look into it more closely. The official report says that she had a high level of alcohol in her blood and that the cause of death was accidental drowning.

From what I know of Heather, none of this adds up."

Edward sat forward with interest. "What do you think happened?"

"I think she was murdered, Edward."

"Oh!" He stiffened visibly. "That's shocking. Why do you think that?"

"Heather did not drink heavily, and as for her swimming naked—have you had any guests, including Heather, who were in the habit of nude bathing?"

He shook his head. "Absolutely not, and I can't imagine Heather doing that either. But why aren't the police taking that into account?"

"Caseload," Paula answered simply. "I know how it goes because Thelo told me about it many times when he was a detective. To be able to close a case quickly as an accident or suicide and not add it to their bottleneck of open homicide cases is like receiving a Christmas present. So when the medical examiner says Heather accidentally drowned because she was drunk, the investigators are only too happy to jump to accepting that."

Edward appeared uncomfortable and worried, and Paula realized that if he had to choose between the two evils, from his perspective the death of a hotel guest from accidental drowning was preferable to murder.

"Do you mind if I see the pool?" she asked.

"No, of course not," he said. "I'll take you. We can get there directly from here."

She suspected he might be wishing she wasn't delving into unpleasantness that wasn't particularly good for business, but as an old friend he couldn't very well refuse her request. She followed him as he unlocked the back entrance door of his office and stepped into the rear courtyard of the hotel where the warmth of the evening hit them like a blast from a furnace. March was one of Ghana's hottest months.

"We've drained it and closed it down temporarily," Edward explained to her as they approached the pool. "We're going to renovate it and make it only one meter deep the whole length. I know you can drown even in a bathtub, but at least one has a better chance of finding one's footing if the pool isn't too deep. I plan to put an extra guard on duty to patrol at night."

The area was barricaded with bright red Keep Out tape, and without the allure of cool, turquoise water, the pool was an uninviting crater. Its gradually increasing depth was indicated along the sides to a maximum of 2.5 meters. The deck was constructed of textured concrete ending on either side in varnished wood trellises mounted with pool lights. Four chaises longues and three sets of umbrella table-and-chairs were distributed around the deck. A bar with a shade awning stood on the right hand side.

"Was she found at the deep end?" Paula asked.

"Right," Edward answered. "Mr. Miedema, one of our guests, discovered the body when he came to do his early morning laps."

"He's the one who tried to revive her?"

"Yes, he did CPR until a doctor we had staying here arrived and pronounced Heather dead."

"Is the doctor still around?"

"No, he checked out the day before yesterday, I believe – went back to the UK."

"What about Mr. Miedema?"

"He's staying until next week Wednesday. If you'd like to talk to him after we leave from here, we can check if he's back from work. That's his chalet over there."

Paula followed his pointing finger about 200 meters away where an earth-red, thatched cottage stood nestled in a thicket of bougainvillea bushes. "Yes, I'd like to do that."

Returning her attention to the pool, she noticed a large, partitioned blue-gray slab on the roof of the structure housing the bar. "Those look like solar panels."

"They are," Edward said. "Mr. Miedema works for a solar installation company and he put in a small system for us last year. The large enclosure at the right is the control station containing the battery and the inverter."

"Impressive," Paula said, trying to sound interested, but she was preoccupied with the haunting image of Heather drowning and the vain attempts to revive her. She shuddered. Naked and drunk? No way.

"Do you have CCTV installed anywhere?" she asked Edward hopefully.

"Ah, if only," he said, shaking his head in regret. "I'm going to have it put in now that this is happened. I'm sorry it's too late for Heather."

"She stayed on the second floor of the hotel, correct?"

"Yes. Room two-sixteen."

"I'm curious whether someone might have seen her go to the pool that night," Paula said. "Has anyone reported that to you?"

"No one has said anything to that effect—not to me, at least. Behind the lobby, there's a private hallway for hotel guests that leads via a locked rear exit to the back garden and swimming pool. To get back in, they use their hotel keycard. So, very late at night when there are no guests around and there's only one attendant at the desk, she could have easily slipped out unobserved."

"I see." She paused. "Edward, do you know of anyone who might have wanted to harm Heather?"

"Not at all," he said, looking mystified. "Everyone liked her and that's why it's hard to imagine anyone hurting her, let alone killing. She was so friendly—maybe even a little too much."

That piqued Paula's interest. "What do you mean?"

"I worried when I saw her chatting with everyone from the housemaids to the gardeners and the security guards. You know, sometimes our people try to take advantage of foreigners who are kind to them."

"Did you ever express that to her?"

"On one occasion, yes," he said, with the slightest of hesitation.

"What was her response?"

"She just smiled and thanked me—said she would be okay."

But Paula was still curious. "Was there someone in particular you were concerned about her interactions with?"

"I didn't like the way Amadu, one of the security guards, used to stare at her and go out of his way to engage her in conversation," Edward said, his distaste showing. "It wasn't his place to do so, and I warned him to stop."

Interesting, Paula thought. "Do you think there was anything more? I mean, something between the two of them?"

Edward seemed repelled by the idea. "No, I don't."

"Is Amadu here today?"

Edward shook his head. "I sacked him."

"Oh," Paula said in surprise. "Because he was being forward with Heather?"

"Not that. I'll explain. The guards are mostly occupied at the front of the hotel—they sit near the sentry box and keep an eye on who comes and goes—but they're also supposed to patrol the rear of the hotel at least once every two hours during their shift.

"Amadu came on duty as usual at nine that Sunday night. He admitted he went to the back around ten but not after that. If he had, he might have found Heather before it was too late, or maybe even before something happened. That's why I sacked him. Neglect of his duties."

An idea leapt into Paula's mind. "Is there any way I could get in touch with him?"

"Sure," Edward said, appearing slightly taken aback. "I can text you his number if you want."

"Thank you. Again, I'm sorry for being so nosy. I'm still so troubled by Heather's death, and I really want to understand."

"No, I agree with you completely," he said, nodding vigorously as he scrolled through his phone contacts. "I'll send you the number now, and then we'll go to see Mr. Miedema."

7

Jost Miedema welcomed them into his chalet, cordially shaking hands with Paula as Edward introduced her. He was a tall, tanned, lean white man with a bony face and a rugged nose that might have been broken at some point in his life. His brown hair, styled with gel, had a few slivers of gray.

"Please, do sit down and make yourselves comfortable," he said, a slight Ghanaian lilt to his underlying Dutch accent. "Can I offer you anything? A soft drink or water?"

His visitors politely declined as they took a seat. The sitting room, carpeted lushly and furnished with soft leather armchairs and dark mahogany side tables, was deliciously chilled by a whisper-quiet air conditioner. The compact, gleaming kitchen was visible on the other side of a small dining section. Paula assumed the bedroom was at the end of a short hallway on the other side of the sitting room.

"This is really lovely," she said to Miedema. "Much more

spacious than it looks from outside."

"Thank you." He patted Edward on the back. "I'm grateful to my dear friend here. He takes good care of me."

"You deserve it," Edward said. "You and your company have been our faithful customers for years."

Miedema looked soberly at Paula. "I know Heather worked with you at the High Street Academy, so I want to say a special sorry for your loss."

"That means a lot to me," she said. "I owe you special thanks as well for trying so valiantly to save her."

"If only," he said with obvious regret. "I've been reliving that morning with nightmares. I felt so futile and despairing as I was trying to bring her back to life, because deep down I knew I was too late. And all the time I was asking myself how this could have happened."

Paula saw his eyes cloud up and she felt moved. "It must have been a terrible feeling."

"It was," he said softly. "You know, we met soon after she had arrived in Ghana. I saw her swimming laps in the pool and I complimented her. We chatted for a while, and when she found out that I'd been a triathlete and swimming trainer, she asked if I would help her work on her stamina and speed. Of course, I said yes."

This was new information for Paula. "You swam together?"

"Most of the time I'd stand at the side of the pool and time her," Miedema said, miming the use of a stopwatch, "or use a camera to take shots that we could analyze later— not that she had a lot to improve on. She was very good, but she was getting even better. We did race every once in a while for the fun of it."

"When did you find the time to do all this?" Paula asked. "I imagine you're very busy."

"In the evenings, mostly. I swim regularly in the mornings, but Heather said that would be too much of a rush for her."

"The papers reported that you found Heather naked," Paula said, finding it awkward to bring this up with a man she had only just met.

He nodded, looking almost as uncomfortable.

"Forgive me for asking so many questions," she said hastily, trying to put him at ease, "but you see, Heather was very dear to us at the Academy. We're all trying to understand what could have happened. The nakedness alone…well, it's just incomprehensible."

He met her eyes squarely. "I understand completely. I've been going over that question in my mind and thinking back over and over about the events on Monday. I woke up at five forty, my usual time. As I got to the pool, I saw her body at the bottom near the deep end. I dived in and within a few seconds I brought her up and out onto the side, where I started to do CPR. But she was cold and stiff, so I knew I was too late."

"Did you notice if her clothing was anywhere around the pool?"

"I could have missed it in the excitement, but I didn't see anything." Miedema looked up at her, cast his eyes downward again and rubbed his brow as if he had a headache. "I don't know how to make any sense of it. Why was she naked in the pool without any sign of clothing around? Even if she was drunk or tipsy, I can't imagine her leaving her room naked. That wasn't like her."

Paula paused before phrasing her next question. "Mr. Miedema, I know this may sound a little strange, but were you aware of anyone who might have wanted to harm Heather? Or even kill her?"

He contemplatively chewed on the inside of his cheek. "Look, I'm not making any accusations, but I think she was having trouble with the gentleman she was seeing. I'm aware he works at your school, Paula, so I don't want to offend anyone."

"You won't," she replied easily. "When you say 'having trouble,' what do you mean?"

"I don't know how bad it was," Jost said, running his fingers through his hair, "but I can tell you that on Sunday evening, when I was coming back to the chalet from dinner at the hotel restaurant, I saw Heather arguing with him near the hibiscus bushes over by the pool—what's his name again?"

"Oliver," Paula said. "Did you hear what they were saying?"

"Not all of it, but at one point Heather said something like, 'I don't want to do this anymore.'"

"He didn't…hit her or anything violent like that?" Paula asked, almost wincing with the fear that the answer might be 'yes.'

Miedema shook his head. "No—not that I saw, at least."

63

She felt relieved. "Did you hear any commotion or disturbance much later that night, by any chance? Maybe by the pool?"

"I wish I had," he said regretfully, "but the way the chalets are built, the two bedrooms are located to the rear, so there could be a pool party going on and I would hear little or nothing."

Lost in their individual thoughts, they were all quiet for a moment until Paula thought of something. "Those solar lights around the pool—are they on all night?"

"Yes," Edward said. "They're set to turn off at six in the morning."

"I understand you installed them," she said to Miedema with a smile.

"Yes," he said, looking pleased. "I work for a small solar power company called Greenlight, based in Amsterdam. We offer cost-effective solar installations to sub-Saharan Africa. I put in solar lighting around the pool last year for Edward. They'll recoup the upfront cost of the system in no time at all without the electricity bills and the headache of the constant power failures plaguing Ghana right now. Hydroelectric power is not the best thing for this country."

"I think I was only half paying attention when Edward was explaining the system," Paula said. "You have the solar panels, the battery, and what else?"

"The inverter," Miedema said, looking happy to discuss his field. "The panels convert the sun's energy and charge the batteries. The batteries discharge to the inverter, which switches the direct current to alternating. That's what powers the lights around the pool."

"Got it," Paula said. "Maybe I didn't notice, but are there are no lights inside the pool itself?"

Edward shook his head. "Not worth the trouble or expense. If the bulbs go out, we have to order them specially and pay a technician to install them. In any case, they attract insects toward the water. It's better to have external lights that draw the insects away from the pool."

"Ah, I see," Paula said. "Very interesting. Learn something every day."

"Now I'm trying to get Edward to go a hundred percent solar for the whole hotel," Miedema said, grinning.

Edward cleared his throat and feigned choking. "Em, that's a little too hefty a bill for us right now."

Miedema laughed. "I'm going to keep sweetening the terms until you can't refuse, my friend."

Paula watched the two men joking around and realized how much they liked each other.

"Do you stay in Ghana for months at a time?" she asked Miedema.

"Two or three weeks, normally. I'll be back in Holland next week Wednesday to be with my kids for a month or so."

Paula noticed he hadn't said wife and kids. "Do you install home solar systems? I'm interested."

"Absolutely," he said eagerly. "Just call me when you're ready and we can set up an appointment at the office."

They exchanged phone numbers and she stood up.

"Thank you very much for your help, Mr. Miedema."

"Oh, no, not at all," he said, standing as well. "And please, do call me Jost."

"Okay—I will."

As Paula got to the door, she turned to him again. "I was wondering—did you ever think Heather was depressed?

Jost turned down the corners of his mouth and shook his head slowly. "Quite the contrary, she seemed unfailingly upbeat. But as I told Chief Inspector Agyekum when he was here on Tuesday, I can't pretend that Heather confided in me to the extent that she would have talked about anything troubling her deep down. We knew each other only in the context of our training, and for a number of good reasons, I liked to keep it that way and I believe she did too."

Probably wise, Paula thought, still wondering about Jost's marital situation. Then an idea struck her. "You said you took snapshots of Heather's swimming technique— might you have one or two photos you could share? One of my staff is putting together a slideshow to honor her, so if you have something that shows her swimming prowess, we'd love to have that."

"But of course! I'm happy to. Shall I send them to your phone?"

"Please do. Thanks again."

Before Paula left, she asked Edward if he would allow her to see the room in which Heather had stayed. Not a problem, he said. The police had released it and it was vacant for the moment.

"Jost seems like a very nice man," she said, as they returned to the hotel.

"He is."

Paula tried to think of a diplomatic way to put her next question. "You don't think...I mean, there's no reason to believe he was involved with Heather beyond the swimming training?"

They had reached the rear entrance to his office and he swiped his card. "Absolutely not," Edward said firmly. "You heard what he said about not getting unduly involved with her. He's an honest guy."

"I notice he mentioned his children but not his wife."

"Yes, he's been divorced for many years."

He picked up a key card from the front desk and they went upstairs to Room 216. A far cry from Jost's chalet, this accommodation had only the basics—one room with a bed, a desk, and a chair. The adjoining bathroom was very small. Nevertheless, everything was clean and neat. Most of Paula's volunteers came to Ghana with limited funds, and the Voyager, with its reputation for cleanliness and affordability, was the perfect hotel for their needs. Edward ran a tight ship.

Paula went to the window where she had a full view of the three chalets. However she noticed that the trellis at the side of the swimming pool obscured most of it. It was possible, then, she thought, that a hotel guest could have looked out of the window in the middle of the night on Sunday and missed Heather's body in the water.

"Nice room" she said, turning back to Edward and smiling at him as they came out. "I like it."

"Thank you." He pulled the door shut. "Let's go this way and I'll show something."

She followed him downstairs. At the bottom, two doors faced them at right angles to each other.

"That one goes to the lobby," Edward said, pointing to the right. He bypassed it. "But if you want to go for a swim, you go out this way."

He pushed open the second door and the exited onto a concrete walkway.

"Oh," Paula said, now comprehending. "It's the same back area you have access to from your office, just from a different exit."

"Right, and this path leads to the chalets and the pool. So, as I told you, Heather could go directly from her room to the pool without being spotted, something I was proud of before because of the privacy it offered the guests. Now that's all changed, and we will have a CC camera that shows who goes in and out of this door."

Paula was staring thoughtfully at the exit door. Perhaps Heather came outside that night to meet someone at the pool without having any intention to swim, and then something went terribly wrong.

"There's absolutely no way to get from the lobby of the hotel to this rear exit without being seen?" she asked Edward.

"I never say never, but it would be difficult. Either the front receptionist or the security guard would spot you."

Paula gazed at the pool in the distance. What happened that night? She was eager to talk to Amadu. She hoped the night guard might know more than he had revealed to his boss.

8

$\mathcal{T}$hat night, after the twins were in bed, Paula and Thelo relaxed in the sitting room and indulged in vanilla ice cream. She hesitated to tell him about her visit with Edward at the Voyager. Despite the rationalizations she had used to justify it to herself, there was no way around it: she had gone "snooping." Thelo would not be happy about that.

"I have some news for you," he said at length, licking cream off his plump lips.

"Oh? What's that?"

"Do you remember the forensic pathologist I used to tell you about—Dr. Anum Biney?"

"Mm. The one you said is so good that all the detectives want him to do the postmortems on their cases?"

"Correct. I thought over what you said yesterday at the office and decided to call Dr. Biney this morning about the case."

"Oh, good!" she exclaimed, thrilled. "What did he say?"

"He couldn't talk long because he was about to do an autopsy, but he promised to get back to me about it this evening or first thing tomorrow."

"Wonderful, wonderful! Thank you so much for doing that, my love."

She gave him an ice-creamy kiss on the cheek, and he laughed.

"I thought he would be the best person to consult," he continued, "because he has insights into both detective work and forensic laboratory studies. He's smarter than all the rest of us put together."

"I can't wait for him to call."

"I need to caution you though, Paula," he said, leveling his spoon in her direction, "Dr. Biney may not tell you exactly what you want to hear. He may side with the conclusions of the pathologist who did Heather's postmortem, and he might say that her blood alcohol level was completely valid. Are you prepared for that?"

"Yes, I am."

"Are you going to accept what he says even if it's not what you'd hoped for?"

"Yes."

His eyes were boring into her, and she had some difficulty meeting his glare.

He grunted. "Okay. You've given me your word. I don't want to hear you backtracking later on."

"You won't," she said, watching him as he got up. "Where are you going?"

"I want more ice cream. Is it really made in Ghana?"

"That's what it says on the carton."

"It's as good as Italian."

"No ice cream is good as Italian," Paula said with conviction. Last year, Thelo had taken her to Italy for a memorable weeklong trip in celebration of her birthday. It helped to have contacts in the travel and tourist businesses. "That's the last I'm buying for the rest of the year," she called out. "You're getting too fat."

"Yes, yes, you've made it plain. Want any more?"

"No, thank you. This is enough."

He came back with another generous serving. "Since you're so concerned about my, em, rotundity, why did you buy the ice cream in the first place?"

"Because you asked me to."

"Doesn't mean you had to agree," he said, sitting down

They both began to giggle.

◆ ◆ ◆

Dr. Biney called as they were getting ready for bed.

"Thank you very much for getting back to us, Dr. Biney," Thelo said, and Paula detected a deferential tone that she was unaccustomed to hearing from her husband. "I'm well, and you? Paula is here with me. Will you mind if I switch to speaker mode so she can join the discussion? Great. Here we go. We're all on now."

"Hello, Paula." Even on the little speakerphone, Dr. Biney's voice was a rich baritone. "How can I help?"

She summarized the case and what concerned her so much about it. "The bottom line, Doctor," she said in conclusion, "is that my colleagues and I knew Heather well, and we just cannot believe that she could have gone swimming naked. Secondly, she did not drink heavily, so it seems impossible that she had a high blood alcohol concentration. Third, she was a very strong swimmer, and was the least likely person to have drowned."

"Your reasoning is sound," Dr. Biney said with his clipped, precise diction. "First of all, let me express my condolences. I read about this in the papers and I find it very tragic indeed."

"Thank you, Doctor."

"But it's fascinating as well," he went on. "Two questions need answering. First is whether the high blood alcohol concentration measured in this unfortunate young woman's bloodstream was representative of her true physiologic state before death, and the second is, did she die by accident or homicide? Do you agree?"

"Yes, absolutely," Paula said, feeling a slight thrill that the doctor's line of thinking seemed, at least to start, in harmony with hers.

"Postmortem measurement of blood alcohol levels is a tricky business," he continued. "One reason is that microbes involved in decomposition of the body can themselves produce a mixture of alcohols, including ethanol."

"Wait," Paula said incredulously. "Doctor, you're saying that the microbes could actually create blood alcohol levels regardless of whether alcohol was in the person's system before death?"

"Correct."

Paula glanced at Thelo, who was himself looking

surprised. "If she was in the water for say, six or seven hours," she asked Biney, "could enough decomposition take place for that effect on blood alcohol to occur?"

"It could, yes. Decomposition is slower in water than in air of course, but this time of the year in Ghana, ambient temperatures even at night are high, and the water in the pool was probably warm as well from natural solar heating during the day. Both those factors will increase decomposition. Once she's out of the water, putrefaction starts to accelerate, so one has to get the serology samples drawn as quickly as possible to avoid errors, even if the body is refrigerated. If it's not done expeditiously, the alcohol levels will rise even more."

Paula's heart was racing. Dr. Biney's eye-opening information was bolstering her case. Out of the corner of her eye, she saw Thelo sitting very still, and she knew that he had not been expecting this at all.

"What about the autopsy itself?" she asked eagerly. "Shouldn't the pathologist have been able to distinguish between homicidal and accidental drowning?"

"That brings us to the second question," Biney said. "A shortcoming of law enforcement all over the world is the tendency to assume that a drowning death is an accident, especially when it takes place in a swimming pool, which is particularly associated with recreation and fun. If Heather's body had been discovered under a bush or even at the side of the pool, everyone from the first policeman on the scene to the pathologist would have a high index of suspicion for foul play.

"Not so with drowning deaths. Signs of struggle may be absent, altered, or difficult to interpret because of the changes induced by hours of immersion in water. So while I don't approve of a hasty rush to the conclusion that a drowning is accidental, the bottom line is that homicidal drowning is a more difficult case to prove, and it's for that very reason that I personally believe that there are many, many more homicidal drowning deaths annually than we realize—not just here in Ghana, but internationally."

"That's a lot of people getting away with murder," Thelo said somberly.

"Indeed," Biney said. "There's something else, too. If Heather was murdered by drowning, it means she would have struggled terribly for a minute or so. That tremendous exertion of the muscles will also accelerate decomposition and bring the alcohol levels up."

"Oh, my God," Paula whispered in horror at the thought of Heather fighting for her life.

"I apologize for being so graphic," Dr. Biney said.

"No, it's all right." She looked at Thelo before going on. "Doctor, is there a chance you could get the case reexamined, and that you could do the autopsy this time?"

Biney hesitated. "Em...I don't think it's an unreasonable request, but in practice we may run up against a lot of opposition, from the pathologist who did the case right up to the Director-General of CID. It will take a lot of persuasion to reopen the investigation, and even then—well, you know how slowly things move over there."

"Yes, we know," Paula and Thelo chorused.

"I'm going to be out of town until next Wednesday," Biney said, "but let me see what I can do when I return. I don't want you to get your hopes up too high, though."

"We understand, Doctor Biney," Thelo said. "Thank you for offering."

"Not at all. If there's anything more I can help with, please feel free to call."

Thelo hung up and looked at Paula.

"Well?" she said.

"I'm flabbergasted," he confessed. "I didn't know all that stuff about the bacteria."

"It validates everything I've been saying," she said quietly. "This was no drowning accident, Thelo. Heather was murdered. Someone has to reopen the case. Should we call Agyekum?"

He frowned. "No, better let Dr. Biney take it up when he gets back—like he said he would."

She looked at Thelo for a long time, pondering.

"What?" he asked. "Why are you looking at me like that?"

"I'm skeptical," she said finally. "Skeptical that Dr. Biney is going to try that hard to reactivate the investigation."

Thelo looked insulted. "How can you mistrust probably one of the most principled men alive?"

"I don't mistrust him at all," Paula denied. "I think he'll make a bona fide argument that the case should be reopened, but if he runs up against opposition, which he himself said he expected to happen, he's not going to fight for it. And when you think about it, why should he? He's busy, he travels all over the country, and his plate is more than full. He doesn't have time to fight for it."

"But the bottom line," Thelo said firmly, "is that he's still our best chance. So, my advice is that we wait until he returns next week and see how he can help refocus attention on the case."

He got into bed, cast around for the TV remote and switched through the channels until he got Al Jazeera English. While he was watching the news, Paula fetched a blank sheet of paper and a pencil and sat up against her pillows next to him. She had learned a few things about detective work from watching him in years past. He had always made lists and diagrams to help organize his thoughts and the facts. She wrote: "Heather Peterson Murder" at the top of the page and underlined it. After a moment's thought, she added,

1. *Heather: A little wine/beer(?) but not intoxicat when she drowned: falsely elevated BAC*
2. *Found naked in public pool—out of character for her*
3· *Murdered—who drowned her? Motive?*

Suspects
1. *A robber who tried to steal her clothes and swim suit, she challenged him, resulting in a struggle?*

Her handwriting was small and most of the sheet was blank, as was her mind. She looked at Thelo, and he took his eyes off the TV screen to lean over to what she'd written. After a moment, he shook his head.

"A robber?" he asked in some amusement. "You learned about enough homicide cases from me to know that the first suspects in a murder are people the victim knows. The reason you can't write anymore is that you're close to the same people Heather was, and that means the suspects you name could be men and or women you care about."

She sighed. He was right.

Thelo switched off the TV and sat up. "Heather was seeing Oliver, right?"

Yes."

"So you have to put his name there along with the motive. What would his motive be?"

Paula wrote,

1. Oliver – rejected lover?

Thelo nodded. "Yes, correct. Who else?"

"Diane," Paula said uncomfortably. "She was smitten with Oliver for a while, and then Heather came along. Diane claims she was already done with him, but that might be sour grapes."

"Agreed," Thelo said. "So, jealousy would be the motive there."

She wrote down,

2. Diane – jealous of Heather? Disgust for "jungle fever"?

"Jungle fever?" Thelo said in surprise. "Like in that

77

movie?"

"Yes. Diane's words, not mine. She looked revolted when she talked about relationships between Ghanaians and white people. I still can't see how she could kill her friend Heather, though. And I can't see Oliver doing it either."

"There you are," Thelo said, a little smugly. "Not so easy when you find yourself investigating people you know and like, is it?"

"There has to be someone else," she said weakly.

"There very well might be," he said, his words beginning to slur in his drowsiness.

"We'll see what Dr. Biney can dig up." She looked at him as his eyes began to drift closed.

"Good night, sleepy-head."

"Mm," he muttered. He was out for the count.

On her sheet of paper, she wrote:

To do
1. Interview Amadu
2. Meet Mr. Peterson
3. ?

Yes, Paula intended to ask more questions. It wouldn't hurt to have Dr. Biney help in any way, but for the reasons she had given Thelo, she wasn't going to hang her hopes on him, and certainly not on Chief Inspector Agyekum. In effect, she thought with irony, she was up against a men's club, men who didn't fundamentally understand why Heather Peterson would not go swimming drunk and in the nude.

9

On Saturday, Thelo had family affairs to attend to, and Paula was to drop Stephan and Stephanie off at their cousins before going off to do some shopping. They were running a little early, so Paula opted to first swing by the General Post Office to pick up some mail. On the way there, they passed through Jamestown, home to most of the students at High Street Academy and probably the oldest part of Accra. It was a jumble of open-air markets, houses with corrugated metal roofs, winding streets and mysterious alleys.

Traffic slowed to a crawl at Ussher Fort. People walked by the decaying edifice without regard for its ancient history. In the next block, in an abandoned, skeletal building that had never gotten past the first floor muscled teenage boys in mismatched shoes or none at all played a sweaty game of soccer under the burning morning sun. Market women with impossible loads on their heads walked the uneven pavements and cut across the street between cars, while itinerant vendors used their best sales tactics to unload trinkets on captive drivers in the paralyzed traffic.

Stephan was beside Paula in the front passenger seat, his head bent studiously over his handheld video game as his thumbs worked. He had begged her to allow him to take the device along and she had relented.

"Five more minutes of that, then you put it away," she told him quietly. "Hear me?"

"Yes, Mummy," he said, looking up at her for a brief moment of acknowledgement.

Paula was undecided whether these games were good, bad, or of no consequence. Facing the reality that she could never stamp out the boy's devotion to them, she limited his playing time. She turned for a second to look at Stephanie, who was in the back seat gazing out of the window with absorption. Physically, she was a female copy of her fraternal twin brother, but she was the gentler and more introspective of the two, often exerting a moderating influence on Stephan, who could easily get out of hand.

A young man with vestigial, crumpled legs rolled up the middle of the street on a skateboard that he propelled with his hands, stopping at each vehicle to beg for some loose change. He and many others like him all over Accra had astonishing traffic negotiation skills, but what they did was still dangerous. As he drew up to Paula's Highlander, he stopped and looked up, reaching up with a hopeful, cupped palm. She lowered her window and greeted him in Ga. "How are you?"

"I try, Madam." He had a brilliant, infectious smile and

a powerful upper body from years of his particular form of locomotion.

She smiled back. "All your life in the street?"

"Since about twelve years old."

"Tough, eh?"

"Very tough, Madam."

She gave him a cedi bill, perhaps ten times what many people would give. His face lit up. "God bless you, Madam."

"Thank you, Sir. And you."

He sped off and zigzagged to safety on the pavement as traffic began to move again. She put her window back up.

"Why is he like that, Mummy?" Stephanie asked.

"He probably had polio when he was a little boy."

"What's that?" Stephan asked, looking up at her.

"It's a disease where the germ goes to your spinal cord and you can't move your legs anymore. So they get small and weak."

"Can we get it, Mummy?"

Paula shook her head. "No, we're all safe, because we had the vaccination at the doctor."

"Oh," he said, looking relieved.

"Is it because he's crippled that he's poor and has to beg for money?" Stephanie asked.

"Something like that," Paula said. "It could be his mother and father couldn't take care of him or didn't want to, so they put him out on the streets and he never got to go to school."

"That's cruel, Mummy."

"Yes, and it reminds us to always be kind to people, no

matter what they look like or how poor they are."

Paula welcomed these discussions. She often fretted that the twins were too sheltered and privileged, too insulated from hardship. Their riding along in an air-conditioned SUV sealed off from the sweltering weather outside was emblematic of that cocooned life. They attended a private international school where they interacted with children of similar status, not the kind of deprived kids who went to High Street Academy. Paula often felt guilty about it, and she had once brought the twins to spend a half-day at Academy so they could experience something profoundly different from their relatively plush school. They had enjoyed themselves and made some friends, and Paula had almost wished Stephan and Stephanie could also spend time with their impoverished counterparts in their cramped, dilapidated Jamestown quarters. But Thelo, less plagued than Paula by these angst-filled existential questions, had vetoed that idea.

Stephan was now watching the soccer match in the abandoned building.

"Anyway," he proclaimed, "I like poor people more because they play much better football than rich people."

Stephanie giggled. "Stephan, you're so silly."

Her brother chortled, and before long all three of them were laughing until their sides hurt.

Once Paula had left the twins with her sister Ama, she went off to continue her errands. She wondered if Mr. Peterson had arrived in Accra last night as he had planned. Midafternoon, while she was at the Melcom supermarket, she received a call from him.

She stepped into a side hallway where there was a less noise. Any Saturday in Accra was shopping chaos. "Okay, that's better. How are you, Mr. Peterson? Did you arrive safely?"

"Yes, thank you."

"Where are you staying?"

"At the Airport Holiday Inn."

"I'm only a few minutes away," she said. "I would very much like to meet you."

"Shall we say in an hour?"

◆ ◆ ◆

A mixture of Ghanaians and white people were drinking and eating in the Holiday Inn lounge when Paula arrived. With a sprawling lobby and a massive, expensive flower arrangement in the center next to a miniature fountain, this was a far cry from the Voyager Hotel. You can just smell the money, Paula thought. Four attendants were busy at the reception desk, compared to Voyager's one or two. Paula looked around for Mr. Peterson, realizing she didn't know what he looked like.

"Paula?"

She turned. "Mr. Peterson?"

"Right. I recognized you from the photos Heather sent us."

"Pleasure to meet you, Sir."

She had imagined him as taller. He was in his late fifties, his hairline withdrawing from his forehead. Paula saw where Heather had inherited her stunning aqua eyes, but his were weary and reddened.

"I'm at that table over there," he said. "Would you like to join me?"

She followed him.

"I'm so sorry that we have to meet under these circumstances," she said, taking a seat opposite his.

"So am I," he said. "But I thank you for coming."

He had finished a soft drink. Paula ordered one for herself and insisted on getting him another with a sampler plate of Ghanaian appetizers. They dispensed with the customary banter about his flight and how scorching he found the weather in Accra.

"I've called Chief Inspector Agyekum's number several times without success," he said.

"Yes, weekends are not the best," Paula said sympathetically, "I'm sure he will get back to you quite soon."

"On Thursday, he emailed me a scanned copy of the conclusions of the autopsy, but I gotta tell you, it looks like a bunch of BS, excuse my language. Why've they been in such a hurry to close this case up and forget about it? My daughter does not drink, nor does she drown in six feet of water."

Paula leaned forward a bit. "Mr. Peterson, I talked to an associate of my husband's who is a forensic pathologist. He wasn't directly connected with this case, but we called him because he's one of the best forensic experts we have in Ghana – not that we have many. Anyway, he told us something I didn't know before. Forgive me for this indelicate language, but the bacteria in a dead person can actually produce different types of alcohol. So, when they measure the blood alcohol concentration in the lab, it might appear that the person drank more than he or she actually did."

"Really?" he said, sitting bolt upright with a new brightness in his face. "That must be it. I knew there had to be some kind of mistake. Could your forensic guy intercede in the case somehow and do the autopsy over?"

"He said he would see, but honestly, I think it's doubtful. In addition, he's out of town until the middle of next week, unfortunately."

"Oh," Peterson said, deflated again. "Forget it. I want Heather out of here before then."

"I see," she said, with a sense of disappointment that Dr. Biney wouldn't get the chance to redeem the investigation.

"I was at the mortuary this morning to officially identify Heather's body," he said despondently. He choked up and attempted to hide it by taking a sip of his Sprite.

"It's hard," she said with feeling. "Very hard."

He looked away from her, desperately trying to stem the flow of tears.

"You also mentioned the FBI might assist the investigation?" she asked quickly, hoping that keeping him talking would help.

"That didn't turn out the way I had expected," he said in resignation. "The agent I spoke to was supportive, but the bottom line is the FBI can't go barging into a sovereign country and start investigating. They'd need the cooperation of the local authorities, and since they're on good terms with the Ghana Police, they don't want to spoil that."

Paula nodded. More or less what Thelo had told her.

"Who is this man called Oliver?" Peterson asked her.

She got the feeling this was one of the uppermost questions on his mind. "Oliver Danquah? He's one of the teachers at the High Street Academy."

"Before I left home, I talked to Heather's best friend, Jody, and she said Heather had told her Oliver was hustling her to help him get to the States. What was going on there?"

"I don't know the details," Paula said awkwardly. "I assume Jody also told you that Oliver and Heather were dating each other?"

Peterson's face twitched as if he'd tasted something unpleasant. "Yes, she told me."

"So, I really wasn't privy to their private discussions," Paula said. "At least, not regarding this particular topic."

He looked bitter and disconsolate. "This whole thing is crazy. It's a nightmare."

"Have you ever been to Ghana before?" she asked him. "Or anywhere in West Africa?"

Peterson shook his head as if he wouldn't have dreamt of it. He looked haggard and battered by grief, bewilderment and jetlag.

"Things are very different here from what you're used to in the States," Paula said. "I realize that it makes what you're experiencing all the more difficult."

"I just want to get out of here and take my daughter with me," he said, his voice trembling.

"Yes," she said wishing she could say something

comforting. "How is your wife taking it? She suffers from multiple sclerosis, Heather told me."

"That demonstrates the level of trust she had in you," he said, with a look of some admiration. "She never talked about Glenda, her mother, except with those she felt close to. A lot of pain there."

"I can imagine. It's terrible to watch a loved one at the mercy of such a disease."

"Not only that," he said. "My wife is ill, no question, but she can be harsh, maybe even manipulative and cruel. It sounds like an awful thing for me to say, but it is what it is. Her relationship with Heather was…rocky, turbulent. They weren't close. I think that's why Heather preferred to avoid the subject altogether." He dispiritedly stirred his Sprite with the straw. "I was hoping one day they would reconcile. Now they will never get that chance."

He let the tears roll down his face and straight into his drink. Paula felt her heart breaking for him, and she made a new vow that, whatever it took, she would find out what had really happened to Mr. Peterson's beloved daughter.

10

She stopped over at her sister Ama's place and sat with her in the shade of the backyard, where the twins were playing with their cousins. A few girlfriends came by and Paula stayed another hour catching up on gossip around town. But then it was time to go and she persuaded reluctant Stephan and Stephanie to get into the Highlander for the trip home.

Thelo was back when they arrived. He supervised Stephan and Stephanie in getting cleaned up while Paula cooked. After dinner, they all had ice cream and watched TV together until it was the twins' bedtime. Paula read them a story, tucked them in with a goodnight kiss and joined Thelo back in the sitting room.

"So, did Mr. Peterson arrive?" he asked her.

"Yes, last night. He's in deep shock. He began to weep and I felt so sorry for him."

Thelo nodded contemplatively. "It's unimaginable – losing a son or a daughter."

They exchanged looks, thinking of the unbearable anguish each would feel if either of their children died.

"But for him, I don't think it's just the loss," Paula said. "It's the notion that she was intoxicated before she died. The implied message of the autopsy is, 'Heather, if you hadn't been so drunk, you would not have drowned,' almost as if she was to blame for her death. And then, she was nude. People think that's shameful, and it's tainting her reputation. Mr. Peterson loathes it, and so do I."

"I realize that. "He scrutinized her. "So, what have you been up to?"

"What do you mean?" she asked evasively.

"Edward called me today. Said you went to see him yesterday evening?"

"Oh, yes," she said, her face getting warm. "I was going to tell you all about it."

"When were you planning to do that?"

"To be truthful, I wasn't sure, because I didn't know how you would react to my going to see him about Heather's death."

"Right, because you had promised—"

"I know I said I would wait and see what Dr. Biney can do about the case next week," she broke in quickly, "but Edward is a friend. What harm was done stopping in to say hello? We haven't seen him for quite some time, anyway."

"But you didn't tell me you were going to do see him," Thelo said tersely.

"Because I hadn't planned on it. It was one of those spur of the moment things."

"Still doesn't mean you couldn't have told me about the visit last night—regardless of what you thought my reaction would be. What's going on with you? We share everything with each other. Why all this secrecy?"

"I'm sorry, Thelo. I don't know what else to say."

"So?" he asked. "What did Edward tell you?"

She gave Thelo a full rundown—how Edward had taken her to see the pool under reconstruction, and then to meet Jost Miedema, who had set up the solar lighting and had been helping Heather with her swimming technique. Both men had expressed concerns about her interactions with men—Edward referring to her "friendliness" across social boundaries, and Jost to her involvement with Oliver. According to Jost, Heather and Oliver had quarreled on Sunday night not far away from the hotel pool.

"But Oliver hasn't mentioned the argument to me," Paula told Thelo. "He said she didn't seem like her usual self on Sunday, but not that they quarreled."

"Are you going to ask him about it?"

"Of course. I need to know what happened."

"But you'll be considerate about his feelings, won't you? Don't make him feel you're assigning blame to him."

"I won't." She paused before continuing cautiously. "There's something else. Edward sacked the night watchman, Amadu, because he didn't patrol the back of the hotel late that night, which Edward said he was supposed to do. Amadu was one of the people Edward thought Heather was over-friendly with."

Thelo shrugged. "You don't fraternize with the servants. Basic rule."

"I don't think that's the way Heather thought about things, though," Paula pointed out. "That was one of the nicest things about her. But what I was thinking was that Amadu might know something he's not telling Edward."

Thelo frowned. "You're not thinking of going to question this Amadu guy, are you?"

She bit her bottom lip and looked at Thelo for a long moment without answering.

"That's what you had in mind, isn't it?" he said.

"Honestly, yes."

"I'm warning you—don't do it."

"Come on, Thelo," she said sharply. "Why not?"

"Because it's going to cause problems. Problems with the police, problems with people who don't like being questioned, and problems with me. We are not in a movie. It isn't safe, and you are not trained in investigation, so leave it to the professionals."

"Professionals?" she echoed. "The professionals have closed the case, have you noticed? And don't try to convince me that they'll magically reopen it. Whether you, Dr. Biney, or anyone else asks them, it's not going to happen. I know how CID works because I watched you for years trying to function within the system. It's like an antique windup car that won't budge, let alone start."

"That's a gross exaggeration," he objected.

"Maybe, but I think my point is made. Either I find out what happened to Heather, or no one ever finds out."

"I like how you flatter yourself."

"Sorry, but that's just how it is," she said fiercely. "I may be an amateur, but at least I care, and I won't sit around doing nothing while this investigation gets buried like a coffin."

Thelo sighed, shaking his head. "You're impossible. I mean, I can't even reason with you." He stood up abruptly. "I've got work to do."

He went off to his study—his sanctuary from me, Paula thought ruefully. That's the way he became when he was peeved with her: he gave her the silent treatment. She didn't like it one bit but what she liked even less was a ominous feeling that trouble was brewing between her and Thelo over her role in the investigation of Heather Peterson's death. He wanted her to back off, but she wanted to do more—much more.

11

After church on Sunday morning, Thelo and Paula took Stephan and Stephanie to the Accra Mall playground, where the twins joined scores of other happy children on the slides and trampolines.

Her phone buzzed and she saw she had a text from Jost. He had attached two pictures of Heather. In the first, she was neck high in the pool, wet hair slicked back away from her face, which was lit up with a radiant smile. Her aqua eyes twinkled in the sunlight, their color made all the more intense by the reflection of the turquoise water. She looked free and lovely.

The second photo was an action shot of her on the upstroke of the butterfly, her dark reflecting goggles just above the surface and the lean muscles of her shoulders in sharp relief. It was a masterpiece. She immediately forwarded the images to Diane, knowing she would love them.

Paula scrolled to Amadu's number, hesitating over it and glancing up at Thelo who was helping Stephan and Stephanie into the train ride. Here goes, Paula thought. Amadu didn't pick up her call, even after three attempts, but a few minutes later he called back, curious about the unknown number that had appeared on his screen. The line was bad. Putting her finger in one ear so she could hear above the clamor of her surroundings, Paula explained who she was and why she had called. He sounded tentative, prompting her to hurriedly add that she had nothing to do with the police.

She asked if she could rendezvous with him somewhere, since they were having trouble hearing each other. After some persuasion, he suggested they meet at Nima Junction and described what he would be wearing.

Her heart in her mouth somewhat, she walked up to Thelo. "I need to go to Nima to meet Amadu."

Incredulous, he stared at her, but she didn't flinch. He made a disgusted noise with his mouth and turned back to the children shaking his head.

♦ ♦ ♦

Paula found it ironic that Amadu had chosen this corner on Nima Road as the meeting place, because it was exactly where the Nima Police Station was located. She got out of the taxi, looked around, but didn't see him anywhere at first. Nima was bustling with its customary bedlam – pedestrians zigzagging between horn-blowing vehicles, market women spilling out onto the pavement, scrap metal dealers pushing their laden trollies, and porters balancing towering loads on their heads.

She was just beginning to worry that Amadu had changed his mind when she recognized him on the other side of the street by his accurate self-description. She waved at him and he crossed over to her.

"Good afternoon, Madam," he said courteously. He was probably about twenty-five. He had a tribal mark on one cheek and bore the leanness of one who can't quite fulfill his calorie needs. He wore a black T-shirt with an image of Rihanna and jeans set well below his slim hips.

A Barclays Bank branch was not far away and since banks were closed Sundays, it was quieter on the side not facing traffic. It wasn't as exposed a spot as Thelo might have advised her to choose, but Paula had quickly sized Amadu up and decided that this was no thug with bad intentions.

"Thank you for meeting me," she said as they stood under the bank's awning for shade. "I don't know if you were able to hear me well when we were talking on the phone, but as I was saying, Miss Heather worked with me at the school on High Street."

"It's terrible what happened to her," Amadu said, his head dropping. "I hear something about they say she drink too much and when she tried to swim, she drown."

"Did you ever see her drink a lot?"

"No, Madam."

"Did Chief Inspector Agyekum talk to you – the detective

investigating the case?"

"Agyekum?" Amadu shook his head. "Not at all."

Her phone interrupted them with the ring tone assigned to Thelo.

"Excuse me," she said to Amadu, moving away a few paces. "Hi."

"Are you meeting with him now?" Thelo asked neutrally.

"Yes."

He grunted. "Everything okay?"

"Everything's fine. He's harmless. Thank you, Thelo." She was pleasantly surprised that he had called and hoped it meant he was relenting on his initial disapproval of her quest. She returned to Amadu. "Sorry about that. So, at what time did you come on duty on Sunday evening?"

"At nine o'clock, then the other security guard go home and I alone am left to work until six in the morning."

"That's your normal shift?"

"Yes please."

"Mr. Edward told me that you went around the back of the hotel around ten o'clock to check the pool area and the chalets."

"Yes please."

"Was anyone in the pool at that time, or near the chalets?"

"No, not at all."

Watching him, Paula got the impression that he was a self-assured young man.

"What about Heather?" she asked. "Did you see her anywhere?"

"Sometimes she used to go to the pool around nine or

ten o'clock time, but I didn't see her that night."

"And so after you patrolled the back, you returned to the front of the hotel."

Amadu nodded. "Yes please. I sit in that sentry box there."

"Mr. Edward told me he sacked you because you didn't return to the pool area during the night."

"Please, Madam," Amadu said, plaintively gesticulating, "only now he say he tell me when I start to work at the Voyager since about four months that make I go around the chalets and the pool every two hours, but please, he never tell me that. He tell me say I can check the place one or two times or something like that or if I think something wrong. Nobody can pass to the pool except the people who stay in the hotel, and those people don't give any kind of problem. In all the time I work there, I never see somebody go to the pool at midnight or one o'clock in the morning, so what am I going to check it for?"

He sucked his teeth in annoyance and distress.

"I understand what you're saying," Paula said. "I agree with you."

Amadu looked somewhat vindicated.

"Do you know a man called Oliver?" she asked. "He was Heather's boyfriend."

"Oh, yeah. Nice man. He always greet me when he see me. That Sunday night he came to see her, and he leave at about eleven thirty."

Paula frowned. "Eleven thirty? Are you sure?"

"Yes, Madam."

That was a definite discrepancy. Oliver had told Gale that he had left the Voyager at eight thirty.

"Did he say anything to you when he was leaving?" Paula asked.

"By that time, I was at the sentry box. When he pass there, he say, have a good night—something like that."

"During the night, did anything unusual happen at the hotel?"

"No, it was quiet. One German man coming from Tamale, he arrive after midnight to stay at the hotel. By that time, Mr. Edward was still there."

"Mr. Edward? You mean, the manager?"

Amadu was puzzled by her confusion. "Yes, Madam."

"He was at the hotel past midnight? What was he doing there so late?"

"Oh, so you don't know?" Amadu laughed. "Sometimes Mr. Edward come there secretly at midnight or even one o'clock in the morning to check we no dey sleep on the job. One time he catch the receptionist sleeping in the back office and sack him on the spot just like that. He say he don't pay us to sleep."

Well, that is true, Paula thought. "What time did Mr. Edward leave?"

"Some time after he greeted the German man. It seem they are friends. Mr. Edward stay maybe about one hour but I didn't see him go, so I don't know the exact time."

"Do you know what time he arrived at the hotel that night?"

"Not at all. You know, he can come and go without us

knowing by a side gate—only he have the key for it. He park outside and come in and you won't know he is there because he can get into his office from the back."

A secret side gate used exclusively by Edward, Paula thought. This was intriguing news, and so was the revelation that Oliver left at eleven thirty, not eight thirty.

"Did you ever see Miss Heather go into Mr. Edward's office for anything?" she asked Amadu.

"Yes, sometimes. Maybe to tell him if something is not working in her room—say for example the toilet have broke or hot water finish. Sometimes he use to go to her room."

An alert went up in Paula's head. "He went to her room? For what?"

Amadu shrugged. "Maybe to ask her if everything was okay. He like her."

"Did he ever spend a long time in Miss Heather's room?"

"Maybe some five or ten minutes," Amadu said. "Or maybe twenty."

That seemed a long time for a manager to spend in the room of a hotel guest. "Twenty minutes? Amadu, are you sure?"

"Let's say ten," he backpedaled.

Paula had her doubts, but she moved on. "That Sunday night, did you see Miss Heather go to Mr. Edward's office?"

"No, Madam. I didn't see her."

"You say Mr. Edward liked Heather. What do you mean?"

He smiled one-sidedly and looked away. "He like her. That's why he sacked me."

"I don't understand."

"Because she always talk to me and make friendly with me. That make Mr. Edward jealous. Because he want her for himself."

Paula considered Amadu carefully. This palm soup was getting thicker by the minute.

"Did he tell you that, Amadu? That he wanted her for himself?"

He shook his head and pushed his bottom lip out. "No, but I can see how he look at her that he want her too much."

"What about you?" she asked. "Did you also want Heather?"

"Me?" he said, pointing to himself in surprise.

"Yes. You."

He began to laugh.

Paula couldn't help smiling. "What's funny?"

"Oh, no," he said, shaking his head. "Allah did not plan for Miss Heather and me to be together. I just like her and respect her. She was very kind woman."

"She was," Paula agreed softly. "Amadu, tell me what happened the morning Mr. Miedema found Miss Heather in the pool."

"It was almost five minutes to six," he began. "I was waiting for the day guard to come and relieve me. Then the desk clerk started to shout at me that someone drown in the swimming pool, so I start to run there. Before I reach, the gardener too run come and talk me say make I call the doctor. So I run to the doctor room and wake him.

"When we return to the pool, Mr. Miedema was pressing on Miss Heather's chest. How the body and the face look like, I never see anything like that before. The arms and the legs"— Amadu bent his wrists and drew his forearms stiffly to his torso—"they be like this. Then the doctor tell Mr. Miedema to stop pumping the chest and he put his hand on Miss Heather neck, and say she have dead already."

Amadu put his hands on his hips and looked at the ground, shaking his head.

"It was a terrible experience, eh?" Paula said.

"Yes, Madam. I feel very bad, because maybe if I went to patrol the back of the hotel during the night, maybe I can save her."

"You can't be in two places at one time," she said. "And even if you went back there every hour, you might still not have been able to save her because it takes only a short time to drown."

"Yes, I know. But…"

She put a friendly hand on his shoulder. "I understand how you're feeling. Me too, I worry if maybe I missed something about Heather that I could have done something about."

He looked warmly at her and smiled.

"Let me ask you something else," she said. "When you went to the back of the hotel at ten o'clock in the night, were the lights on around the pool?"

He nodded. "Yes please."

"And I know they normally stay on all night. I wish at least someone looked out of his or her hotel window that night. Maybe they might have seen something."

"But, Madam, I think say the lights went out sometime

during the night. Or somebody turn them off."

Paula looked at him sharply. "Why do you say that?"

"When I first run to the pool that morning, I see the lights already turn off. By that time, it was four minutes before six. Normally they suppose to go off at six, automatic."

"How could someone turn off the lights?"

"You switch off for the inverter. You can use the on-off switch, or if you like, you can press the reset and the lights go come on again automatic at the next cycle."

"You know how to do that?"

"Yes, and Mr. Edward too."

"Oh," she said. "Mr. Edward too. Besides him and you, do you think anyone else at the hotel knew how to turn off the inverter?"

"No. Mr. Edward, he don't like too much people to know, so only he and the night security guard they can do it."

"I see." She reflected on that a moment. "Amadu, thank you."

She had guessed he was from northern Ghana, so she thanked him in her rudimentary Hausa, which made him smile broadly in appreciation.

"Listen," she said, going into her purse, "you've really helped me and been very patient. I know you've lost your job and things are hard. Let me give you a little something to help you in return, okay?"

"Thank you, Madam. May Allah bless you."

"And you."

As Paula walked back to the street to pick up a taxi, she was gratified she had spoken to Amadu. She liked him, but more than that, she believed him, and he had given her a couple jewels of valuable information. A serious new and fundamental question now arose: Was Edward having a secret affair with Heather, an affair gone bad? Had he lusted after her, only to be spurned? Had he turned off the pool lights that night, and if so, why? The underlying question was critical: could Edward have killed Heather?

12

$\mathcal{B}$y the time Paula made it back to the mall, Stephan and Stephanie were more than ready to eat at the food court. Paula firmly turned down their request to dine at the new McDonald's.

"We ate at the one on Oxford Street only last week," she said sternly. "That's enough to last you for months. We didn't have all this cheeseburger stuff when I was your age."

"Did they have Oxford Street when you were our age?" Stephan piped up brightly.

"Yes, we did, as a matter of fact," Paula said with some indignation. "I'm not that old."

Stephan nudged his sister and they both began to giggle.

"Oh, it's funny?" Paula said in mock outrage.

"It's Sunday," Thelo said sullenly to her. "Why not treat them to McDonald's?"

"Don't you start, Mr. Cholesterol," she said. "You need to take off some weight yourself."

He rolled his eyes, but didn't argue. Paula thought he might be thawing out a little toward her, but there was some way to go. They agreed to eat at Papaye, a wildly popular and always crowded restaurant that served a delicious variety of roasted chicken, savory rice and coleslaw.

While Thelo helped the twins with their choices, Paula excused herself and walked quickly down the mall promenade, which was packed with youngsters flirting or sitting around texting—or both. She was looking for the shop where Oliver had bought Heather her swimsuit as part of his effort to cheer her up that last Sunday of her life.

Paula found it—a store called "Sun and Sand," which obviously catered more to expatriates than Ghanaians, who aren't that much into swimwear, anyway, she reflected. A couple of bored young assistants were inside the otherwise empty store and seemed relieved to have something to do as Paula went in and introduced herself. She asked if they remembered a slim, young white woman and a Ghanaian man coming in on the previous Sunday to buy a tangerine-colored swimming costume, as Oliver had described it, but neither of the assistants had worked that day.

"Do you think you still have that outfit?" Paula asked.

"I think so," one said. She went to one of the carousels and looked through the hangers. "Maybe this one?"

She held it up and handed it to Paula. It fitted the description and the quality was excellent, although it was a little too bright for her taste and made for women with much trimmer hips than hers.

"Will you like to try your size?" the girl asked.

"No," Paula said, suppressing a laugh. "I just wanted to

105

see what my friend said she bought last week. Thank you."

On the way back to the restaurant, Paula called Gale.

"Come into work a little early," she told her. "I've just been talking to Amadu, the watchman on duty that night. He told me some interesting things we need to discuss."

◆ ◆ ◆

It was Paula's turn again to put Stephan and Stephanie to bed. They chose one of their favorite Ananse stories and leaned against her on either side as she read. By now, she could almost recite the thing by heart. As she was tucking Stephanie into bed, the little girl suddenly asked, "Mummy, are you and Daddy angry at each other?"

Oh, dear, Paula thought. Nothing escaped the notice of her sensitive daughter. "Why do you ask, sweetie?"

She shrugged. "I don't know. I just thought you were."

"Well, sometimes, even though Mummy and Daddy love each other a lot, they have disagreements. But everything will work out fine, okay? Don't worry."

"Okay, Mummy."

Paula kissed her daughter on the forehead.

"It's just like when Stephanie makes me angry in the nighttime but then I like her again in the morning," Stephan declared in a muffled voice from somewhere underneath his bed.

"Stephan!" Paula exclaimed. "What are you doing under there?"

"I lost a Lego, Mummy."

"You can look for it tomorrow," she said sternly. "You just had your bath and now you're crawling around on the

106

floor? You're going to get dirty."

"Found it!" he yelled triumphantly, his little hand shooting out from under the bed with the recaptured piece of Lego.

◆ ◆ ◆

Thelo was in his study working at his laptop. He didn't look up as Paula came in and sat down in the chair closest to his desk.

She eyed him for a moment. "Stephanie just asked me about what's going on between you and me."

"Mm-hm. And?"

"I responded that we were having a little disagreement but that we'd soon get over it."

"Okay."

"Okay, so can we talk about it now?"

He looked away from the computer, but still not directly at her.

"I know you felt I excluded you when I went to see Edward," she said, "and for that, I'm sorry."

"But then you went and talked to Amadu today after my advising against it," Thelo pointed out. "You had asked me to call someone at CID to see if the case could be looked at again. I thought about it and decided you were right, so I contacted Dr. Biney, because although he's not a CID employee as such, his work is highly respected and he's very influential. Everyone listens to him. But after our long discussion in which he promised to try and help next week, you go just ahead and do what you had been planning to do in the first place. So what was the point of the whole exercise? Why did I even bother?"

"It's still of value," she insisted, "and I really appreciate that you called him. We could do with his assistance. But there are questions that bother me personally, and that I can't rest until I get the answers to, questions that men may not be quite as sensitive about—like why Heather was naked in that pool."

"I see. So I suppose now that you've spoken to Mr. Amadu, you have the answer?"

"Well, no, I don't. But he still had some interesting information."

"Go ahead," he said in a supercilious tone she loathed but forced herself to ignore. "I'm listening."

She swallowed. "For one thing, he thinks the only reason Edward sacked him is because Heather was very friendly toward him."

"Toward Amadu?"

"Yes. He says Edward was jealous of him."

"I would expect Amadu to say something like that," Thelo said, snorting with contempt. "Obviously the boy is bitter about his dismissal and is trying to cast aspersions on Edward."

"Could be," Paula said, but doubtfully. "Also, it appears the pool lights were off for some period overnight and only Amadu and Edward knew how to switch them off."

"Which suggests to me that, if anyone, Amadu is the suspect. I hope you're not suggesting Edward had something to do with Heather's death."

Paula hesitated.

"You're telling me you're taking the word of some low-class, illiterate watchman over that of a trusted friend of ours?" Thelo asked in disbelief. "If Edward had been jealous of Heather's friendliness with Amadu, he would have sacked the boy long before her death. It's clearly because Amadu messed up on his job that he was sacked. Don't believe people just because they seem honest and earnest. They are some of the worst liars."

Paula saw an opportunity to turn this conflict around. "That's why I need you, Thelo. To show me the pitfalls. Can you help? If you're behind me, I can't go wrong."

He let out his breath sharply in frustration. "Paula, the point is that it's not our job. I'm not a detective anymore. I run a business. You're not a detective either. I can't back you up on something for which you're not trained and that could, at least in theory, involve dangerous criminal elements. The very best we can do is what we've already done: ask for help from an expert, Dr. Biney."

They were silent for a while, the hum of the air conditioner the only sound in the room.

"At this point," Thelo took up again, "I don't trust you, and I tell you, it's not a good feeling. I'm even afraid you're going to do something foolhardy like go to Edward and accuse him to his face of foul play."

"I'm not going to do that."

"Oh, I'm so relieved to hear that, Detective Paula."

That was the last straw. She stood up to leave the room. "I'm tired of your sarcasm." At the door, she stopped. "I feel you think I'm somehow undermining your authority. That isn't my intention at all, but you should know that I'm not done asking questions. I can't stop now."

He ran his hand over his baldhead and down his face, a gesture of exasperation that Paula knew well. The wall between her and her husband was now frozen solid.

♦ ♦ ♦

Early the next morning, Paula told an eager Gale about the meeting with Amadu. The first noteworthy revelation was that he had observed Oliver leave the hotel Sunday night at eleven thirty.

Gale drew in her breath. "Is Amadu sure? Oliver said eight thirty."

"Amadu is positive, and I don't think he's lying, either."

"So let me get the timeline right," Gale said, "Amadu came to work at nine that night."

"Yes."

"He went to the back area of the hotel at ten and did a patrol, and that was the only time he did that for the whole night."

"Correct," Paula said. "Let's say he got back to the front of the hotel—the lobby or the sentry box—ten to fifteen minutes later."

"A little more than hour after that, at eleven thirty," Gale continued, "Oliver comes out of the hotel and goes home. Did Amadu see Heather around anywhere at that time?"

"I asked him that too. No."

Gale leaned against the wall with her arms crossed, worry all over her expression.

"Why would Oliver say eight thirty if he really left at eleven thirty? What if this Amadu is mistaken, or even lying? Why do you trust him more than Oliver?"

"Amadu has no reason to lie."

"He does if he killed Heather."

Paula pressed her lips together. "That's exactly what Thelo suggested. And he's furious with me for turning my suspicion on Edward Laryea."

"Edward Laryea!" Gale exclaimed in surprise. "You're suspicious of him now?"

"I have some cause to be," Paula said. "Amadu said he saw definite signs of Edward's attraction to Heather, including sometimes going up to her room for quite a while to check if everything was okay, so to speak. Heather was very friendly toward Amadu, however, and he's convinced that Edward was jealous and sacked him for that reason."

Gale frowned. "The ramblings of a misguided young man, if you ask me."

"Perhaps," Paula conceded, "but there's more. Edward was at the hotel until past midnight on Sunday. Amadu says he sometimes makes surprise appearances at the hotel to check if his workers are doing their jobs the way they're supposed to. While he was there, a German guest— apparently a friend of Edward's—checked in late after a long road trip from Tamale. Edward welcomed him to the hotel and stayed there for some time after that, although we don't know exactly how long."

Gale was studying her. "Okay. Go on."

"I think it's strange that when Edward and I talked about Heather's death, he didn't mention that he had been around the hotel late that Sunday night."

"He might not have thought it was that important."

"How could it not be important?" Paula demanded. "He

was at the hotel on the same night Heather was killed, and he doesn't once remark on it, not even in passing? Gale, that's simply strange."

"So now you believe Edward and Heather were having an affair that went wrong," Gale challenged skeptically, "or that he lusted after her, she turned him down, and it came to a head on Sunday night?"

"Listen to me," Paula said steadfastly. "On Monday morning when Amadu ran to the back of the hotel after hearing that someone had drowned, he noticed that the lights around the swimming pool had gone out. They're set to turn off automatically at six in the morning, but it was a few minutes before, and Amadu is certain about that. So, we can speculate that the lights were off for at least some portion of the night either because of technical failure, or because they were deliberately turned off. Who would have wanted to do that? The murderer, because he needed the cover of darkness to commit the crime. Apart from Amadu, guess who else knows how to turn the lights off and on?"

"Edward."

"Correct. So let's say Heather goes to Edward's office around eleven forty-five Sunday night—"

"What for?"

"Maybe he wanted to see her, or maybe she wanted to see him. While she's in his office, some kind of argument develops between them."

"About what?"

"I don't know—that he loves her and wants her, and why does she reject him and insist on being with Oliver? Edward wants to make love to her in the office. She refuses his advances. In the middle of the argument, the German man arrives from Tamale sometime past midnight, and the front desk calls Edward to let him know his friend has arrived. Edward goes out to greet him, telling Heather to wait a few minutes until he returns.

"After he welcomes his friend, Edward goes down to the pool, turns the lights off, and then returns to the office. He asks Heather to take a walk with him down to the pool, so they can talk more, but really, what he plans to do is kill her."

"Don't you think it would be difficult to persuade her to go with him after they've just had an argument?" Gale asked.

"Edward can be very persuasive."

Gale closed her eyes and repeatedly traced her eyebrows with her thumb and index finger, which she did when she was deep in thought.

"My goodness," she said heavily, opening her eyes again. "I never thought we'd come to this."

"What?"

"Suspecting our friends and associates. Oliver, Edward – maybe even Diane?" She shook her head. "It's horrible."

"I know," Paula said, but not with quite as much despondency. "Thelo is afraid I'm going to confront Edward and accuse him of murdering Heather."

"Are you?"

"No, but I would like to confirm if there's any truth that he lusted after Heather."

"How will you find that out?"

"I thought I might ask Jost Miedema if he knows, or if he

113

observed anything of interest."

"You trust him?"

"Yes. He's an honest observer."

"Okay." Gale sighed. "Meanwhile, what shall we do about Oliver?"

"We need to get the truth from him about what time he left the Voyager that night."

Gale was uneasy. "We do it together?"

"I would like us to, but if you would prefer not, it's no problem."

"I'll do it with you" she said resolutely. "So long as you take the lead."

They looked up as Diane came in with her laptop.

"I have a surprise for you," she said, beaming.

"What's that?" Paula asked.

"I'll show you."

The three women sat together in front of the screen and Diane turned it on and went to iPhoto. For a moment the screen was dark as soft music began, and then faint letters became visible, spelling out the title, Heather Peterson:

Still in Our Hearts;

At work;

Outings;

Fun in the sun;

The slideshow went roughly in chronological order starting from the very first snapshot of Heather emerging from the arrivals hall at Kotoka International Airport. Paula and Diane had been there to meet her. The background music of the collage changed according to the theme and captions, and each photo faded smoothly into the next.

The first set, At Work, had a jaunty score and showed Heather supervising the kids, taking a break to wipe off her sweaty face, piling a bunch of laughing students on her lap, taking part in a tug o' war contest, or hanging out in the office talking or posing with Paula, Diane, Gale and Oliver.

In Outings, Diane had captured Heather on the infamous Kakum National Park canopy walkway stretching from one soaring tree to another. Heather was firmly staring ahead, refusing to look down into the plunging depths.

The music switched again for Fun in the Sun: Heather drinking out of a freshly cut coconut at a Cape Coast beach, pulling funny faces at the camera with Diane, executing a handstand, and making a two-person pyramid by standing on Oliver's shoulders. After the beach collection came photos of Heather at the barbecue Paula and Thelo had held for the Street Academy staff about a month before.

"This next part was hard," Diane said. "I wasn't sure if I should include it, but swimming was something that Heather loved, so I did in the end."

Diane had become teary, and Paula saw why. There was Heather in the Voyager pool, where she was eventually to die. She was lovely against the turquoise water that matched her eyes lookin up happily at the camera. In another, Oliver was sitting next to her at poolside, he muscular and handsome, and she tan and lean in a black swimsuit.

When the next photo came up, Paula asked Diane to pause it for a moment. It was a poolside photo of Heather in the same black bathing costume with Diane, Oliver, Jost, and Edward. Everyone was smiling and Heather looked especially happy.

"That's a really nice one," Paula said. "Who took it?"

"The bartender. That was only about three weeks ago."

"I really like it."

Finally came the two shots from Jost that Paula had forwarded to Diane. As the last photos played and the music died away, Paula felt her own tears pricking, and put an arm around Diane.

"That was lovely" Gale said, dabbing her eyes with a handkerchief.

"It was," Paula said. "Thank for doing that, Diane. I'd like you to show it to the children if you wouldn't mind."

"I'd love to."

"It would also be nice for Mr. Peterson to see it," Gale suggested.

"I think so too," Diane said. "I can email it to him."

She put the laptop away and the three women got ready for work. All through the morning, Paula was thinking about the upcoming confrontation with Oliver and very much dreading it.

13

$\mathcal{T}$he day was over and the kids had gone home. Oliver had agreed to meet with Paula and Gale after classes and he came into the office at a few minutes after two. They sat with each other in a triangle. Paula had chosen not to sit behind her desk because it acted as both a physical and psychological barrier.

"So," he said, "what's up?" His demeanor was both wary and falsely cheerful.

"Whatever comes out of our discussion today," Paula said, "remember we care about you, Oliver, okay?"

"Why," he said with a nervous laugh. "Am I in trouble?"

"Something I need to ask you," Paula said. "You said you left Heather at the hotel on Sunday night around eight thirty, correct?"

"Right," he said, but now he didn't sound quite so sure. "Around there."

"Yesterday, I talked to Amadu, the security guard who was on that night. You remember him?"

"Yes, I often saw him when I went to the Voyager."

"He told me that you left the hotel at eleven thirty, not eight thirty."

He stared at Paula for a moment, and then he looked at Gale and back at Paula. The two women waited for his response for what seemed like several minutes. "Amadu is both correct and wrong," he said finally.

"How so?" Paula asked.

"I did leave the hotel at eight thirty to visit my father at Korle Bu hospital, but then I came back again to see Heather about two hours later. I stayed only about forty-five minutes and then left again. That's when Amadu saw me. Diane did too."

"She did?" Paula asked, surprised. "Where was she that she saw you?"

"She was in the lobby talking to one of the clerks when I came down from Heather's room, and ever since last week Monday, she's been looking at me with suspicion. In fact, when we had the staff meeting on Friday, you might have noticed that strong stare she was giving me."

"I did," Paula said, "and I was wondering what was going on."

"It's as if she was asking me with her eyes whether I had done something wrong," Oliver said.

"Have you?"

"No, Paula."

"Why didn't you admit that you went back later to see Heather?"

"Because I was afraid it would have seemed suspicious." He dropped his head. "Maybe I'm a coward. I'm sorry."

"You're not a coward," Gale said, reaching out to squeeze his hand.

"A lot happened that Sunday, didn't it?" Paula said to him.

"I confess I only told you some of the story," he said despondently. "What I said about Heather being unusually quiet was true, but what I didn't tell you was that we quarreled that evening."

That concurs with Jost's story, Paula thought.

"I loved Heather," Oliver continued, "and she said she loved me. I wanted us to be married and I told her that many times. But she could never say yes to me, and I couldn't understand why. On Sunday evening when we went for a walk in the hotel garden, I asked her if she could write a visa request letter to the U.S. embassy officially inviting me to the States. She said the process is not as easy as all that, and I asked her why she wasn't willing to try. I asked her, is it because you don't want to see me again after returning to the US?"

"Then she became annoyed and started to tell me all kinds of crazy stuff. She said she didn't want to do this anymore, and I said, what do you mean? She said she had been told how so many young Ghanaian guys like me try to take advantage of American girls and use them to get visas, or to marry them so we can become US citizens, and I was shocked. I asked her who told her such a thing but she wouldn't say. It really pained me." He touched his chest over his heart. "And me too, I have a hot temper and I began to quarrel with her. She turned her back on me and ran into the hotel."

Paula was visualizing what must have been quite a dramatic scene.

"After a few minutes," Oliver continued, "I went to her room and knocked, but she didn't answer, so I called her on the phone three or four times. She still didn't respond. Then I tried to talk to her through the door, but she told me to go away. I sat in the lobby for a while, not knowing what to do, but I had to leave at eight thirty, because I had promised my father that I would visit him in hospital. I think by that time, Amadu wasn't yet on duty, so he didn't see me leave."

Paula was watching him closely. Knowing his mannerisms well, she felt he was telling the truth—so far.

"I stayed with my father for about one hour," he went on, "but all the time I was thinking about Heather and the argument. I was very confused. She had hurt me, but at the same time, I started to feel bad about the things I had said to her. When I was leaving the hospital, I called her again and told her how sorry I was and that I wanted to see her again that night. At first she said no, but I begged her over and over, and she agreed. So I went back."

He folded his lips inward, as if the next part of the story was going to be the hardest to tell. "Heather told me we had to have a serious talk. She said she liked me very much, and that she enjoyed sex with me, but in her heart, she didn't believe we were made for each other and so she didn't see her future with me. I asked her if she had someone waiting for her in the States, and she said not at the moment. So I asked her, what shall we do next? She said we should give each other some space and not see each other romantically any more. We can work together, but not sleep together. That's how she put it. I felt as if I had been stabbed through my heart. I was sad, but I was angry, too, because I felt she had wronged me for no good reason."

He lowered his head again. Gale got up and stood beside him, gently rubbing his shoulders. "Tell us what happened next, Oliver."

He shrugged. "That was the end."

"The end?" Paula asked.

He nodded. Stunned, the two women exchanged glances. They did not want this to be the resolution, nor Oliver the culprit, but they both knew that the confession they had feared most was imminent.

"Then you persuaded her to go down to the pool with you?" Paula asked softly.

He looked up at her, puzzled. "What do you mean, go down to the pool?"

She was confused. "You didn't go…take her to…"

"Take her to where?" he said with another shrug. "There was nowhere to go anymore. We shook hands and agreed to end our relationship then and there, but not as enemies. I said good-bye to her and returned home. Like Amadu said, by that time, it was about eleven thirty."

14

Oliver had departed, leaving the two women both relieved and embarrassed.

"I jumped to conclusions," Paula said, wincing. "I thought he was saying he killed Heather."

"So did I."

"We made a mess of the interview."

"I don't suspect him anymore," Gale said.

"Neither do I, and now I feel terrible that I suspected him."

"Boss," Gale said hesitantly, "this may be a sign that we have to let this go. Maybe we have this wrong. I mean, I loved and respected Heather, but—"

"But maybe she did go swimming in the nude?" Paula cut in. She shook her head firmly. "In fact, I believe I can prove to you right now that she did not do that."

She picked up her phone and dialed Mr. Peterson.

"How are you, Sir?"

"Frustrated," he said sharply. "How does anything get done in this country?"

"Is there something I can help with?"

"I spent the whole morning and part of this afternoon just trying to reclaim Heather's belongings," he said angrily. "Why is this so difficult? I went from one department to the next, filling out I don't know how many forms. Half the time, people weren't in their offices and I kept being told to come back tomorrow. I had to get someone from the embassy to apply pressure before I finally got my hands on her clothing."

"So you have them now?"

"Yes."

"I'm sorry it was so vexing," Paula said. "You shouldn't have to go through all that."

He blew his breath out sharply in exasperation.

"Where are you at the moment?" she asked.

"Back at the hotel with a stiff drink. I couldn't take it anymore. I was sitting at CID supposedly waiting to speak to the Director-General, and after about an hour someone decides it would be nice to let me know that he wasn't even in. Jesus Christ."

"I sympathize. Even us hardened and jaded Ghanaians go insane over the way we often conduct business. Did you have a look through Heather's things?"

"Yes," he said, his tone softening. "It was bittersweet. I would never have imagined how even small items could come to mean so much."

"So true. By the way, you may not know this, but Heather

had two swimsuits: a black and a tangerine."

"Tangerine—really?" He paused as if he was thinking something through. "Only the black one is here."

"Only the black one." Paula gave a thumbs-up to Gale. "Just as I expected. You understand the significance of that, Mr. Peterson?"

"It's just struck me," he said, as he began to laugh with sudden relief. "It means she didn't go swimming naked. I knew it!"

"So did I," Paula said happily. "Mr. Peterson, we're going to reclaim Heather's good name. I promise you that."

"Thank you," he said with feeling. "I can't tell you how much I appreciate your championship of my daughter."

"She only deserves it," Paula said. "Do you now have a date of departure set?"

"This Friday—Saturday at the latest."

She had a sudden idea. "Before you leave, High Street Academy would like to honor Heather's memory. Can you visit us on Thursday afternoon for an event?"

She was already organizing it in her head: the children could stage singing, traditional Ghanaian dancing and drumming, spoken word performances, and other tributes to Heather—perhaps a little theatrical performance as well. Several of the boys were naturally talented acrobats who loved to put on a show. Yes, it will be good, she thought. In Ghana, when one honors a person who has passed on to the next world, it isn't all doom and gloom, because one is celebrating her life as well. Paula might even be able to get one of the local Jamestown marching bands to perform.

They would be glad to. Finally, they could screen Diane's wonderful tribute. Paula's heart leapt at these thoughts. "Can you come, Mr. Peterson?" she pressed eagerly.

"Okay," he said a little hesitantly. He probably didn't know quite what to expect. "Yes, sure, why not?"

"Wonderful," Paula said. "I'll call on Wednesday evening to confirm."

As she rang off, she beamed at Gale. "Vindicated," she said with satisfaction.

Gale smiled. "You win, boss. I shouldn't have doubted Heather that way. And what was that you were saying about an event?"

"We're going to put together a beautiful sendoff for Heather and her father. Get all the staff in to start the planning. We have two days to rehearse."

15

$\mathcal{B}$efore Paula left for home that afternoon, she called Jost to ask if she could swing by his office to learn a little more about solar installations for the home, and also to ask him another question in private.

"Actually I'm not in Accra right now," he told her. "I'm down at beautiful Cape Three Points taking a couple days off, but I'll return tomorrow."

"And you're leaving for Amsterdam Wednesday morning?"

"Correct."

"I see," Paula said. Tuesday, the following day, would be packed with meetings for her, including a dreaded one with her boss. "What about if I come to the hotel tomorrow evening?"

"Yes, that would be perfectly fine. I'll be back by then."

She spent the next few minutes revising the list she had started on Friday night. It had expanded considerably.

1. *Heather – A little wine/beer, but not intoxicated when she drowned*
2. *Homicidal death, not accidental*
3. *Black swimsuit with her belongings, but not the tangerine => Heather was wearing it when she went for a swim => she was not naked*
4. *Where is the tangerine swimsuit—murderer took it?*
5. *Pool lights out—murderer switched off the inverter?*

Suspects
1. *Amadu—motive? – knows how to switch off lights*
2. *Edward: spurned lover? Also knows how to turn off lights.*
3. *Oliver – more and more doubtful as a suspect.*
4. *Diane – jealousy? Disgust for "jungle fever" Doesn't seem a likely suspect.*

No. 1 & 2 know about the solar system, inverter, etc prime suspects?

Her phone rang, and she was surprised to see that it was Chief Inspector Agyekum calling.

"Good afternoon, Chief Inspector."

"Afternoon, Madam." Long pause.

"May I help you?"

"Yes, please, Madam, Mr. Djan called me today to inform me that you are very concerned about the investigation of Heather Peterson's death and that you still believe there has been foul play."

"Yes, that's correct," Paula said. She was thrown a little off balance by the unexpected call, but she wasn't going to squander this opportunity to reinforce her case. "As I explained before, Heather did not drink. Dr. Biney has explained to my husband and me that a falsely elevated lab test could have been created during the decomposition of Heather's body, so that's why it appeared that she had been drinking heavily when in reality she had not. And now that we know that one of her two swimsuits is missing, it is almost certain that she was wearing it when she went swimming—not naked as previously thought."

"I see," he said blandly. "That's interesting. However, our forensic lab is quite confident that the obtained result is correct. Anyway, no problem—as your husband said, when Dr. Biney returns, he will discuss all these things with us and then maybe we will take it to the Director-General for his input. So, don't worry, we will handle it."

"So, you'll reopen the case?" she said hopefully.

"Like I said, Madam, we will handle everything, so don't trouble yourself to try and investigate the case. For your own safety and the public interest, we don't advise that. Am I clear?"

"When can I find out whether the investigation has been reopened?" she persisted.

"We are looking into it. Madam. I must advise you not to interfere any further with the procedures of the CID, or there may be problems."

His voice had turned hard and flat, and now Paula understood he wasn't reassuring her. In fact, he was warning her away.

"Interfere?" she echoed in astonishment. "You can only

128

interfere with something if it's actually being done, Chief Inspector. All I see CID doing is a whole lot of nothing."

"Thank you, Madam. Please, we will handle it. Okay?"

He hung up. She was angry as she speed-dialed Thelo's number.

"So, you had Agyekum call me to threaten me, is that it?" she asked him as soon as he came on the line.

"What are you talking about?" Thelo said, sounding bewildered.

"He just spoke to me and warned me not to 'interfere' with CID's work. Did you ask him to do that?"

"No, of course not," Thelo responded indignantly. "I only told him about your concerns, that you had obtained new information from different sources, and that Dr. Biney planned to look into the facts of the case and possibly request it be reopened. I wasn't asking him to call and threaten you at all. Is it my fault that he did that?"

"I guess not," she said sullenly, calming down. "Sorry."

He sighed. "Paula, what's gotten into you?"

"Do you believe Agyekum is really willing to take a second look?" she asked, ignoring his question.

"I don't see why not." Thelo sounded preoccupied. "Listen, I have a meeting. I have to run."

For a while, she sat thinking about the two conversations she had just had. It was tempting to be reassured, but she knew better. Agyekum was simply stalling her. He wanted her to go away and disappear, but she wasn't going to. Instead, she would keep probing until she found her answer, and no one—not Agyekum, Biney, or even her husband— would hold her back.

16

$\mathcal{A}$s Paula had expected, Tuesday was an awful day. Between 8 a.m. and late afternoon, she had meetings in widely separated parts of town. The last of them, and the least welcome, was with her boss. It wasn't until almost 7:30 p.m. that she was able to free herself from his claws. She felt bone tired as she got into the Highlander to face the ride home, then remembering that she had planned to stop off at Jost's place. She called him first to be sure he had returned from Cape Three Points.

"I got back a couple hours ago," he said cheerfully. "I had a wonderful time and I feel rejuvenated. Would you like to come by? I have some pamphlets for you about different home solar systems. And you said you had another question to ask me?"

"Yes, I'll explain when I arrive. No guarantee what time I'll get there, though—what with the traffic."

"That's perfectly fine. I'm not going anywhere. I always just relax on the night before I leave."

"What airline tomorrow?"

"KLM, of course."

She chuckled, and after hanging up with Jost, she called Thelo, who had picked up Stephan and Stephanie from school earlier on and was getting them ready for bed.

"Are they behaving?" she asked.

"They're okay," he said, his tone still somber with her. "Stephan is having his bath, Stephanie is moody about something – don't ask me what."

"Kiss them both for me. I won't be back before they've gone to sleep."

"Why, where are you going now?" he said, sounding a little irritated.

"I have to catch Jost Miedema before he goes back to Amsterdam tomorrow."

"Oh. Still on this solar energy thing, are you?"

"Yes. I am." She wasn't going to tell him that she also planned to ask Jost about a possible Heather-Edward connection.

He sighed resignedly. "I'll see you later, then."

Paula could feel that the air between them had not yet cleared. The sooner she solved this case, the better, she thought. Then life could return to normal.

She made it to the chalet by 8:25, which was a little better than she had anticipated. Jost opened the door at her knock.

"Paula, how are you? Come in, come in. Take a load off your feet. Would you like some wine or a soft drink?"

"Just water will be fine, thank you. I hope I'm not disturbing."

"Not at all. I was just finishing up my packing."

After some small talk, Jost went through the home solar installation pamphlets he'd set aside for her and explained the different plans and options.

"I'm very impressed," she said after studying them. "I'll take these with me and show them to Thelo, my husband, and then we should stay in touch by email—perhaps set something up for when you're in town again, hopefully soon?"

"Probably in July," Jost said. "Now, you said you wanted to ask me about something?"

"Yes, I did, but I also don't want to put you on the spot, so if the question makes you uncomfortable, just let me know and I'll go away."

He smiled. "I doubt that will be necessary."

Paula was about to begin when the doorbell sounded.

"Oh, do excuse me," Jost said apologetically. "It might be Edward coming to say good-bye."

Her stomach flipped. Edward? She hoped not. That would be awkward.

Jost went around the corner to the door and she listened as he greeted the visitor. To her relief, it was a woman who spoke.

"Good evening, Sir!"

"Hi, Selina."

"Please, Sir, I was wondering if you wanted to settle the bill this evening or you will do it in the morning?"

"I can come up a little later tonight, if you like."

"Okay, that will be fine. I'm going off duty, but I'll let all the front staff know. I hope you've enjoyed your stay with us again?"

"I always do. There's one thing I'm unhappy about, however."

"Oh, dear! What's that, Sir?"

"The very last day I'm here is the day Edward fills the pool back up."

As Jost and Selina laughed, Paula realized he was only making a complaint in jest.

"No, truly," Selina said, "I'm sorry for the inconvenience to you of the pool closure, but as you know, after the tragedy, we're trying to minimize the chance that it could ever happen again."

"But of course," he said. "I absolutely understand."

"Thank you, Sir. Isn't it so sad?" she said, her voice softening. "Such a beautiful young woman. Did you meet her father by any chance?"

"No, I didn't, although I would have liked to have given him my condolences."

"He was here yesterday to speak with Edward. He looked devastated.

"It must be very hard for him," Jost said. "Different types of tragedies have struck the two women in his life that he loves the most. His wife Glenda suffers from the most terrible multiple sclerosis, and now his daughter Heather has been taken from him."

" My goodness. How awful."

They moved on to chatting about Jost's children, Selina asking whether he would bring them along on his next visit to Ghana. But Paula's mind was back at Jost's comment on the Peterson's wife and her suffering. How had he known about that? Mr. Peterson had remarked to Paula that with the exception of those she felt close to, Heather never talked about the psychologically painful subject of her mother and her illness. Jost had told Paula when she had first met him that Heather didn't confide in him about anything troubling her "deep down". So why would she have shered details with him about her mother when that was such a difficult topic to discuss? Was Jost hiding something about this relationship with Heather, and if so, why?

Paula's thoughts went quickly from one point to another like billiard balls bouncing randomly off the sides of the table, and at the end of it all she looked down at the solar pamphlets in her hand and realized how stupid she had been all along not to see the connection.

She looked down the hallway leading to the bedrooms. She was sure Jost's conversation with Selina wouldn't last much longer, but she had to take this chance now because she would never get it again.

She moved quickly down the hall. The first door was the bathroom, the second was one of the two bedrooms. She went in and switched the light on. A stylish, fawn-colored suitcase on the bed was almost fully packed, but the top was open. She was about to go through the contents when she spotted Jost's laptop on the desk connected by a USB cable to a Nikon single reflex camera. Forget the suitcase, she thought, quickly crossing the space between the bed and the desk.

The laptop was the same MacBook Paula used, so she

was quite familiar with it. She swiped her finger across the touchpad and the screen woke from sleep mode directly into iPhoto. It was obvious Jost had been downloading images of the beautiful scenery he had captured at Cape Three Points from the Nikon to his Mac.

Paula scrolled through the alphabetized picture albums on the left-hand side, clicking on one called HP. Not Hewlett Packard, but Heather Peterson. The photos were dated from earliest to latest. Scores of action images of Heather's freestyle, breast, back and butterfly strokes. Some posed pictures were included as well, rather similar to the one Jost had texted Paula—a smiling Heather looking vivacious and pretty in the swimming pool.

But then the nature of the photographs changed abruptly, and Paula's blood ran cold. She was looking at several night shots of Heather floating face down in the water in her tangerine swimsuit. Dead?

There was a video. Paula's breath trembled as she clicked on it. The undulations of the pool's surface looked like moving crescents of black and white. Slowly and steadily, Heather, her white skin lit up against the dark, liquid tomb around her, drifted naked to the bottom of the pool.

Paula let out a stifled cry and took a step back, nearly jumping out of her skin as she bumped against someone behind her.

"What are you doing in here?" Jost said. He sounded both horrified and furious.

She tried to turn, but could not. With quick, overpowering strength, he had her in a chokehold.

"I beg you, don't scream, Paula," he pleaded. "I don't

want to hurt you. Please."She stayed still, rigid, and mute.

"We're going to the bed together," he instructed, his voice shaking. "I'll be right behind you to guide you. When you get to the night table, open the drawer. You will see a roll of duct tape, which you will remove and hand to me."

He was breathing heavily as they went in tandem to the bedside and she did as he had instructed.

"Lie face down on the bed with your arms by your sides," he said.

As she lay flat next to his suitcase, he removed his grip on her throat, but the pressure of his knee in her back compressed her chest and prevented her from moving or taking a good breath for a scream. She heard the harsh crackle of the tape as he pulled off a length. He wrapped it around her mouth several times. She felt a sudden panic that she might suffocate, and she struggled for a moment until she found herself quickly exhausted.

"I'm sorry," he said, sounding as if he was about to cry. "I really like you, Paula, but now that you know I drowned Heather, I just can't let you go."

He brought her wrists behind her back and bound them.

"Is it too tight?" he asked her.

She nodded vigorously, trying to say yes through the gag.

He hesitated. "Okay, I can loosen it a little bit, but not too much."

After doing that, he wrapped her knees and ankles.

He got off the bed and began to pace at the foot of the bed. Paula swiveled her eyes to watch him. Muttering to himself in Dutch, he stopped several times and ran his hand through his hair, appearing nerve-wracked and uncertain what to do with her.

"*Godverdomme*," he swore, standing in front of her. "Why did you have to get into all this pointless detective stuff, Paula? Why couldn't you just leave things the way they were? I mean, you're very clever, but what you've done is the height of stupidity. *Mijn God*, just look at the mess we're in now. "

He cursed and paced several times more before pulling up a chair in front of her. He sighed in exasperation and stared at her for a moment.

"Okay, look," he said finally, "I need you to be relaxed and peaceful." He jumped up. "I don't want you struggling."

She looked up at him, eyebrows raised, pleading with her eyes. What was he planning to do with her? If only she could speak, she might be able to reason with him. He went out of her sight to his desk behind her, and she heard him open one of the drawers. For a moment there was silence, and then he came back and got onto the bed.

I'm going to give you a heavy dose of diazepam," he said. "It will make you sleep. I sometimes use it myself in small amounts to relieve muscle spasm after a long swimming session."

He pulled down her waistband, exposing the upper portion of her right buttock. "Here it comes."

She flinched as he stabbed her and injected the stinging medicine.

"It will simply be easier for both of us," he said. "I don't want you to fight me. You're bigger than Heather—more powerful, too. I simply have no choice, Paula. I have to drown you too."

17

*I*t was almost 10 p.m. Gale had texted Paula but not heard back from her. Now her phone rang and she thought for a moment it was her boss calling back, but it was Thelo asking if she knew where Paula was. He'd been calling and texting her to no avail.

"I tried to reach her myself earlier on," Gale said. "I assumed the text didn't get through or she just hadn't seen it."

"Did she tell you she was going to see the Dutch guy at the Voyager?" Thelo asked.

"Jost? Yes, she wanted to ask him if he knew whether Edward and Heather were having a relationship."

"What?" Thelo said, his tone alarmed. "She didn't tell me that. She said she was going to talk to him about solar power installations."

Solar power. Gale went rigid. Jost Miedema had installed

solar lights at the hotel swimming pool. He knew how to turn them on and turn them off.

"Thelo," she said urgently. "I think Paula might be in trouble. I'll go to the Voyager right now, and meanwhile is there someone at CID you can call and have them get over there as quickly as possible?"

"Will do, and I'll see if Paula's sister can come over and watch the kids. I'll meet you at the Voyager as soon as possible."

◆ ◆ ◆

In the darkness of the sitting room, Jost watched from the window as the night security guard made the second of his routine rounds at the rear of the hotel, swinging his flashlight back and forth. Ever since Heather's death, Edward had put an extra guard on duty overnight and mandated that he must patrol the back of the hotel every hour. This one dutifully went to the pool, where the lights were on, looked around and left, making one more sweep of his flashlight before returning to the lobby.

Jost moved quickly, exiting his chalet and running around the back of the other two. He approached the pool from its rear side and went to the control station, where he switched off the inverter. The lights went out and he ran back to his chalet in darkness.

In preparation, he had sat Paula up in a chair in the sitting room.

"It's time," he told her quietly, slipping off his clothes and leaving on only his swimming briefs.

Still in a drugged state, she moaned softly and her head lolled forward as she dozed. He slipped his arms around her upper torso, interlaced his fingers behind her upper back and smoothly pulled her up against him as he stood up, a technique he had learned as a young nursing aide. He lowered himself so that she flopped forward over his left shoulder and then he stood up straight. Holding her legs fast, he left the chalet again, once more circling around as quickly as he could to the swimming pool. In the darkness he gently lowered Paula onto the pool deck, unbinding her wrists, ankles and finally, her mouth. He saw the whites of her eyes as they fluttered open. She murmured something unintelligible.

"I'm really sorry, Paula," he whispered. "Forgive me, but I have to do this."

He got into the water and lifted her in with him. "Goodbye, Paula."

He pushed her head under.

The security guard burst out from the rear entrance of the hotel with Gale right behind him. The pool was in darkness. He switched on his flashlight and Gale followed him as he took off at a run. His beam found a man standing inside the pool while holding down a feebly moving body underneath the water.

Jost's head jerked up as he saw two figures running toward him. He leapt out of the pool.

"Get him!" Gale screamed.

♦ ♦ ♦

The security guard on his tail, Jost made a dash for the rear perimeter of the premises. Gale leapt into the pool, and as tiny as she was, she pulled Paula up before her body began its slow trajectory to the bottom. Her head in free air again, Paula's eyes popped open, she drew in a wheezing breath and began to cough and splutter.

"It's okay, boss," Gale said breathlessly. "I got you."

♦ ♦ ♦

Chief Inspector Agyekum stood over Jost Miedema, who lay prone on the ground in handcuffs. The security guard had tackled him and wrestled him to the ground, keeping him pinned until Agyekum arrived.

At poolside, Paula sat with a large hotel towel wrapped around her as Thelo cradled her in his arms. She was breathing heavily and shivering.

He kissed her. "I don't know what I would do if I lost you."

18

$\mathcal{P}$aula sat forward in the hospital bed of her private room as the doctor listened to her lungs with his stethoscope.

"You're lucky and you have a strong constitution," he said. "Your heart and lungs are fine."

"Thank you, Doctor," she said, sitting back against her pillows.

"Actually," he said folding up his stethoscope, "your assailant did you something of a favor by administering the diazepam. He wanted to make it easier to drown you by making your muscles too weak to struggle, but that also allowed you to conserve energy, and because the drug suppressed your respirations, you didn't inhale significant amounts of water."

If you say so, Paula thought. Thanks to another effect of the drug, she remembered nothing of the harrowing experience.

"Shall I call your visitors back in?" he asked her.

"Yes, please. Thank you again, Doctor."

Thelo, Gale, Diane, and Oliver returned to her bedside.

"Don't tire her out too much," the doctor warned.

Thelo kissed Paula on the cheek and she smiled wanly and held his hand.

"How do you feel?" he asked her.

"Surprisingly hungry."

"Well," he joked, "seeing as how you didn't show up for dinner last night."

Paula laughed weakly, and then winced as a muscle somewhere reminded her she was far from back to normal.

"Thank you for what you've done, boss," Oliver said quietly. "You've honored Heather's name and found her killer too."

They gave her a round of applause.

"Now can we get back to our normal routine life?" Thelo said dryly.

"I think so," Paula said.

"What do you mean, think so?" he asked suspiciously.

"I mean, yes," she responded hastily. "When will Stephan and Stephanie get here?"

"I just spoke to Ama. She's on the way with them."

"Any word on how long you'll be out, boss?" Diane asked.

"I don't plan to stay here long," Paula answered.

"Don't rush it," Gale advised. "Not to worry, we'll hold down the fort."

"Diane?" Paula said. "Can you continue Ajua's tutoring after school and keep a special eye on her? She needs our support. You know how much she loved and idolized Heather, and I don't want her backsliding."

"Of course, I will, Paula."

"How are the rehearsals going for the show?" she asked eagerly.

"A little chaotic," Gale said, "but the kids are doing a fine job. It's going to be a great show."

"I know it will," Paula said.

"Come on, Oliver, Diane," Gale said, "let's go. There's a full day of school ahead."

"Thank you, guys," Paula called out as they left.

Thelo plumped up her pillows. "Get some sleep, now."

"Okay. You leaving for a while?"

"No, I'll be right here."

She woke hours later to Thelo's soft voice. "There's someone here to see you, honey."

Paula looked to her side. Mr. Peterson was smiling at her. "How are you?"

"Better, thank you."

"I didn't want to leave without saying goodbye and thanking you from the bottom of my heart."

She smiled and held out her hand. He took it and gently squeezed.

"Have all the arrangements been made?" she asked.

"Yes, we're leaving Friday, and I must say that everyone has been wonderful. Things have gone smoothly after that rocky start and Heather's all set for the flight back home."

"Good, I'm glad. I was worried you would go away with the most awful impression of Ghana and its people."

"No, not at all. But I do have one little piece of advice:

guys, you gotta pick up the pace just a tad."

She laughed with him. "Point well taken. Thank you for coming to Ghana and watching over Heather."

"Goodbye, Paula, and God bless. Get better real soon."

The nurse came in with a light meal, which left Paula hungrier than before. Thelo went out on a secret mission to get her some "real food." Minutes after he had left, with a light tap on the door, Chief Inspector Agyekum came in.

"Good afternoon, Madam," he said, smiling. They shook hands. "How are you faring?"

"Much better, thank you. Please have a seat. My husband stepped out for a moment."

Agyekum pulled up a chair. "I must say, I owe you an apology."

"Oh?" she said innocently.

"I didn't believe your convictions about Heather. You were right, I was wrong, and I'm sorry I didn't listen to you."

She smiled. "In many ways, I don't blame you. You were going on past experience and you didn't know either Heather or me."

"I'm glad you persisted, however."

"Thank you."

"Not that I'm glad you had to tangle with a dangerous criminal and end up in the hospital," he added quickly. "Not that part."

They laughed.

"Has Mr. Miedema confessed?" she asked him.

"He has, and if I can have your assurances that you will keep it confidential, I will tell you what he said."

"Yes, of course."

"Mr. Miedema fell in love with Heather Peterson probably the first moment he saw her at the hotel swimming pool not long after she got to Accra," Agyekum began. "The way he has always told the story is that when she learned he was a triathlon champion, she asked him to help her improve her stroke and stamina. In fact, it was the other way around. He suggested it rather to her, and after some discussion, she thought it was a good idea. On the pretext of analyzing her swimming style, he took pictures and videos of her performance supposedly to instruct her on how she could improve. He gave her the false impression that he was taking only a few photos, but in fact he took hundreds of them with his high-speed camera."

"Did he begin to make any amorous moves on her?" Paula asked.

"Not for some time," Agyekum said, "but Mr. Miedema felt that she saw him only as her informal coach, an older athlete with the benefit of years of experience, and he wasn't satisfied with that. He wanted a romantic relationship with her. He often spent hours looking at the photos he had taken of her and fantasizing about how he might become her true love."

"So he was steadily developing a dangerous obsession," Paula observed.

"Yes," Agyekum said, "but there was one big problem: Oliver. Sometimes Jost would watch him playing around with Heather in the pool. That made him crazy with jealousy, and he began plotting to separate the couple. He tried to gain Heather's trust, and little by little she became more free with him—maybe regarding him as kind of a fatherly figure. One day, when he asked her about her parents, she poured out her troubles about her relationship with her mother, who is sick with multiple sclerosis. Heather told him she rarely shared that with anyone, and he felt proud that she had confided in him.

"Then he began to slowly poison her mind about Oliver, persuading her that he was using her as a cash machine and a means of getting a visa to the United States. His tactic must have worked, culminating that Sunday when she and Oliver had a big argument and decided they should part ways."

"She trusted Mr. Miedema," Paula said, seeing it clearly. "Trust is a powerful tool. That's how he was able to sway her against Oliver. Miedema knew how to inspire trust while lying to your face. I know that because I myself fell victim to his deception."

"If only Heather could have seen through it the way you eventually did," Agyekum said. "The trust she had in Miedema then became something in his mind that didn't exist in reality. His fantasy was that Heather ending her romance with Oliver meant she was turning to Miedema as her new love. When she called him to say she had broken free, as he called it, he invited her down for some champagne to celebrate. He told me in the interview that it was possibly the happiest day of his life in a very long time. After they had talked a while, he suggested they go for a swim and look up at the stars, which were brilliant that particular night.

"Heather went back up to her room and returned in a new tangerine swimsuit Miedema had never seen before.

He thought she looked lovely in it and asked her where and when she had bought it. She told him it had been a gift from Oliver. His whole world changed in a second. He said to me that he felt as though he had been slashed across the face with a machete. He asked Heather why she was wearing a gift from a man she hated, to which she replied that she didn't hate Oliver at all. They had parted ways romantically because she did not see her future with him, but it wasn't the same as hating him, and although she was no longer going to sleep with him, she was still going to work with him at the school."

"Jost had misinterpreted Heather's breakup with Oliver," Paula said.

"He had," Agyekum agreed. "When he and Heather went out to the pool, he turned off the lights—but not to kill Heather, as you might be thinking. It was so that they could see the stars better. But all the time they were in the nice warm water looking up at those stars, he could not stop thinking about the tangerine swimming outfit. It was eating his soul, but it was what happened next that delivered the full shock to him. Heather suddenly blurted out that she thought she had just made a mistake — that she had been too hasty with Oliver and now she wanted him back."

It must have shattered Jost's whole, elaborated fantasy," Paula said.

"He told me he felt like he was being buried alive. He became frantic, telling Heather he couldn't bear it if she left him, that he loved her and wanted to be with her forever — that he was even planning to fly her to the Netherlands to visit with him. Then, according to him, Heather's behavour abruptly changed at that point. He describes her as becoming hostil and telling him she wouldn't dream of being in a relationship with an old man like him, that she would prefer Oliver any day."

"I dont't beleive she said it that way," Paula interjected, shaking her head. "Knowing Heather, I doubt that she was anything less than tactfull with him."

"I'm sure you are right, Mrs. Djan. Whatever she said, Heather excussed herself and began to leave the pool. Miedema says he felt, even heard, something snap in his mind, and he hit her hard across the side of her head. It knocked her back, and for a moment she was speechless. But then she tried to scream and he became even more enraged. He pushed her underwater and never let her up again. Her writhing, her resistance to him was like pouring fuel on a fire. The more she fought him, the more he wanted to kill her."

Her hand over her open mouth, Paula was transfixed by the vivid picture of terror and violence that Akyekum was painting.

"Miedema claims he barely remembers the struggle," the chief inspector said, "and that it was like a dream. When it was all over, he was dazed, but he remembers walking back to his chalet, fetching his camera and returning to take a picture of Heather's body in the water. The tangerine swimsuit troubled him, so he removed it and took a final photograph and video of her naked. He said it was a hauntingly beautiful image, and although he kept urging himself to erase the evidence from his computer, he was unable to do it. He was always wanting to look at it just one more time."

"Hauntingly beautiful," Paula echoed with a shudder. "How sad. How sick."

"Yes, Mrs. Djan. Mr. Miedema spent the rest of that night thinking that the body would be spotted and the police would soon be knocking on his door, but when morning came and he went to the pool, there Heather was, just as he had left her, and he realized that he had escaped detection-atleast he thought he had, and there begun his subter fuge. Which would have worked, had it not being for you. You should be proud, madam."

"Thank you," she said, "but not proud. Just glad."

19

$\mathcal{N}$o one at High Street Academy was expecting Paula's return to school on Thursday, but she had vowed that she would not miss the tribute to Heather even if she had to be carried there in a stretcher. Against the protests of both her doctor and Thelo, she had signed herself out of Korle Bu on Wednesday night.

Thelo insisted on taking her, telling her she was crazy if she thought he would let her drive herself to High Street Academy. Then Stephan and Stephanie got wind of the upcoming students' performance and begged to join Paula and miss half a day of their own school.

Paula had two stops to make before their final destination, however. Thelo pulled up in front of the Voyager and waited in the car with the twins as Paula went in. The desk clerk told her Edward was in his office and waved her through. She knocked at his door.

"Paula!" he exclaimed as she came in. "What a sight for

sore eyes. Wonderful to see you again. How are you doing?"

"Very well, thanks, Edward. Well, actually I feel a little wobbly, but it will pass."

"Oh, dear, oh dear," he said, concerned. "You mustn't do too much. Please, have a seat."

He guided her to the most comfy chair and sat opposite her.

"Thank you," she said. "And what about you? I know you were very fond of Jost. How are you holding up?"

He cocked his head thoughtfully to one side. "Of course, it's been painful for me, but as the proverb says, when the delicious meal goes bad, you don't want to eat it anymore."

She nodded. "You are pragmatic, and that's why you're a successful hotel manager."

"Oh, I don't know about that," he said, laughing. "Is there anything I can help you with, dear Paula?"

"I certainly hope so. I'm here to make an appeal."

"Of course."

"The turning point in Heather's case was due in large part to Amadu and his powers of observation. At the very least, I think he deserves to be rehired."

"I see," Edward said, considering it for a moment. "All right, that's fair. I'll call him this morning."

"Thank you. One other thing, though. He should be officially recognized and rewarded."

Edward raised his eyebrows. "What do you mean—some kind of award ceremony?"

"That's fine," she said brightly. "In fact I think that's a nice idea. It will build up morale again at the hotel.

Unfortunately, however, ceremonies don't pay bills. A raise is what he needs."

He groaned. "Ah, Paula, you're killing me."

"If it wasn't for him, a murderer might have gone scot free," she pressed. "Come on, Edward. Have a heart. The boy is in need."

He sighed. "Okay. I'll see what I can manage."

"Thank you. You're an angel."

◆ ◆ ◆

Her second stop was at the Ghana Herald building, where she found John Prempeh in his cluttered office.

"Ah, Mrs. Djan!" he exclaimed, jumping up. "To what do I owe this exceptional pleasure?"

He hastily cleared a stack of documents off a chair and offered it to her before sitting down again at his desk. "I understand you were involved in quite a bit of excitement at the Voyager Hotel."

"Yes, I was," she said evenly. "Would you like the exclusive story?"

Prempeh's eyes lit up. "Well, yes. Are you offering it to me?"

"Interested?"

"But of course."

She smiled generously. "Then you shall have it. On one condition, though."

He looked wary. "What's that?"

"That you run an editorial refuting all the lies you told about High Street Academy."

"What lies?" he asked innocently.

"Don't play with me, Prempeh. You know exactly what I mean."

"I don't think I can run such an editorial."

"Fine," she said, standing up. "I have a friend at the Graphic, your rival paper. They'll be happy to get the story and run the editorial against you. Especially when they find out who the so-called reliable source was for your article."

Prempeh's right cheek twitched. "What do you mean?"

She leaned across his desk until her face came unnervingly close to his. "You think I haven't figured it out? The Thursday the pathologist's report came out about the supposedly high levels of alcohol detected in Heather's bloodstream, you wanted some background on it to spice up your story, so you got in touch with Jost Miedema to see if he had some additional information. That was perfect for him, because he realized that if he could strengthen the falsehood that Heather drank heavily and drowned by accident, the case would quickly be closed and further ensure that he escaped detection. Am I right so far?"

Prempeh, his eyes wide and his jaw clamped tight, said nothing and tried to move back from her.

"So," she continued confidently, "on condition of anonymity, Miedema fed you the lie that Heather was severely depressed because of an oppressive workload and terrible working conditions at the Academy. And you happily printed it without making an effort to verify the facts. Now, how would you like the whole world to know that your reliable source is an accused murderer? What is that going to do for the reputation of John Prempeh and the Ghana Herald?"

He swallowed. "Tell me what you have in mind."

"I've already written the editorial," Paula said, stepping back and reaching into her briefcase. "All you need to do is post it."

She handed it to him and he grasped it gingerly using only his thumb and index finger like pincers—as though the two pages were an explosive device. He read it through with visible discomfort. The editorial apologized for misrepresenting the facts about the Academy, touted the school's many achievements, and set the record straight about Heather. She had been happy, had not been overworked, was not depressed, and had not drunk herself to the point of dangerous intoxication. Nor had she accidentally drowned. She had been murdered, and the accused had been captured.

Prempeh sighed heavily. "I'll have to run it by the chief, and do a bit of editing."

"You tell me now which edits you're going to make," she said firmly, still not trusting him. "I have time."

He wanted to change some words and phrases around, and since none of the adjustments significantly altered the message of the piece, Paula agreed to them.

"Can I have your story now?" Prempeh said hopefully, pushing his glasses up his nose.

"Call me when your boss has approved the editorial and it has been printed," she said pleasantly, "and then we'll meet and I'll tell you all about the Voyager Hotel murder and how I solved it."

◆ ◆ ◆

As they got closer to the school, Paula felt more and more eager to see her students again. Stephan and Stephanie were chattering excitedly with each other, both hoping to meet some of the friends they had made during their first visit to the Academy.

When they arrived and got out of the car, Thelo took the twins by the hand and held them back with him a little as Paula went on ahead. She rounded the corner closest to the office and met with the sight of all her students in the yard perfecting their performance of a traditional Ga sea shanty as Gale conducted them. Their voices trailed off as they saw her, Gale spun around to see what they were staring at, and then pandemonium broke loose. The kids jumped up and down for joy, and yelled, "Madam Paula! Madam Paula!" She opened her arms wide, and they ran to her for one big, collective embrace.